The Right to Be Different . . .

"Listen to me," Michael said. "They're taking this very seriously indeed. They're badly alarmed over us. Usually if a Deviation gets clear of a district they let him go. But what's got them so agitated about us is that nothing shows! We've been living among them for twenty years and they didn't suspect it. We could pass for normal. So a proclamation has been posted describing the three of you and officially classifying you as deviants.

"That means," Michael continued, "you are non-human and therefore not entitled to any of the rights or protections of human society. Anyone who assists you in any way is committing a criminal act, liable to punishment. In effect, it makes you outlaws. Anyone may shoot you on sight. There is a small reward if your deaths are confirmed; but there is a much larger award if you are taken alive."

"I don't understand," Rosalind said. "If we promise to go away? . . ."

"That's not enough. They are afraid of us."

Suddenly there was nothing to do but mount the greathorses and ride into the unknown for their own survival and for the future of man.

Also by John Wyndham
Published by Ballantine Books:

OUT OF THE DEEPS

THE MIDWICH CUCKOOS

TROUBLE WITH LICHEN

RE-BIRTH

John Wyndham

A Del Rey Book

BALLANTINE BOOKS • NEW YORK

A Del Rey Book
Published by Ballantine Books

 Published in the United States by Ballantine Books, a division of Random House, Inc., New York, and simultaneously in Canada by Ballantine Books of Canada, Ltd., Toronto, Canada.

Library of Congress Catalog Card Number: 55-9098

ISBN 0-345-27450-4

Manufactured in the United States of America

First Edition: May 1955
Sixth Printing: May 1978

First *Bal-Hi* Printing: October 1965

Cover art by Michael Herring

Chapter One

WHEN I WAS QUITE SMALL I would sometimes dream of a city—which was strange because it began before I even knew what a city was. But this city, clustered on the curve of a big blue bay, would come into my mind. I could see the streets, and the buildings that lined them, the waterfront, even boats in the harbor; yet, waking, I had never seen the sea, or a boat. . . .

And the buildings were quite unlike any I knew. The traffic in the streets was strange, carts running with no horses to pull them; and sometimes there were things in the sky, shiny fish-shaped things that certainly were not birds.

Most often I would see this wonderful place by daylight, but occasionally it was by night when the lights lay like strings of glowworms along the shore, and a few of them seemed to be sparks drifting on the water, or in the air.

It was a beautiful, fascinating place, and once, when I was still young enough to know no better, I asked my eldest sister, Mary, where this lovely city could be.

She shook her head, and told me that there was no such place—not now. But, perhaps, she suggested, I could somehow be dreaming about times long ago. Dreams were funny things, and there was no accounting for them; so it might be that what I was seeing was a bit of the world as it had been once upon a time—the wonderful world that the Old People had lived in; as it had been before God sent Tribulation.

But after that she went on to warn me very seriously not to mention it to anyone else; other people, as far as she knew, did not have such pictures in their heads, either sleeping or waking, so it would be unwise to mention them.

That was good advice, and luckily I had the sense to take it. People in our district had a very sharp eye for the odd, or the unusual, so that even my lefthandedness caused slight disapproval. So, at that time, and for some years afterward, I did not mention it to anyone—indeed, I almost forgot about it, for as I grew older the dream came less frequently, and then very rarely.

But the advice stuck. Without it I might have mentioned the curious understanding I had with my cousin Rosalind, and that would certainly have led us both into very grave trouble—if anyone had happened to believe me. Neither I nor she, I think, paid much attention to it at that time; we simply had the habit of caution. I certainly did not feel unusual. I was a normal little boy, growing up in a normal way, taking the ways of the world about me for granted. And I kept on like that until the day I met Sophie. Even then, the difference was not immediate. It is hindsight that enables me to fix that as *the* day when the first small doubts started to germinate in my hitherto plain field of acceptance.

That day I had gone off by myself, as I often did. I was, I suppose, nearly ten years old. My next sister, Sarah, was five years older, and the gap meant that I played a great deal alone. I had made my way down the cart track to the south, along the borders of several fields until I came to the high bank, and then along the top of the bank for quite a way.

The bank was no puzzle to me then; in common with the rest of the landscape, it simply existed, it just *was*. It had no significance; it was far too big for me to think of as a thing that men could have built. It had never occurred to me to connect it with the wondrous doings of the Old People whom I sometimes heard about. It was simply the bank, coming round in a wide curve, and then running straight as an arrow toward the distant hills—just a part of the world, and no more to be wondered at than the river, the sky, or the hills themselves.

I had often gone along the top of it, but seldom explored

on the farther side. For some reason I regarded the country there as foreign—not so much inimical, as outside my territory. But there was a place I had discovered where the rain, in running down the far side of the bank, had worn a sandy gully. If one sat in the start of that and gave a good push off, one could go swishing down at a fine speed, and finally fly a few feet through the air to land in a pile of soft sand at the bottom.

I must have been there half a dozen times before, and there had never been anyone about, but on this occasion, when I was picking myself up after my third descent, a voice said, "Hullo!"

I looked around. At first I could not tell where it came from, then a shaking of the top twigs in a bunch of bushes caught my eye. While I was gazing at it the branches parted, and a face looked out at me. It was a small face, sunburned, and clustered about with dark curls. The expression was somewhat serious, but the eyes sparkled. We regarded one another for a moment, then:

"Hallo," I responded.

She hesitated, then pushed the bushes further apart. I saw a girl a little shorter than I was, and perhaps a little younger. She wore reddish-brown dungarees with a yellow shirt. The cross stitched to the front of the dungarees was of a darker brown material. Her hair was tied on each side of her head with yellow ribbons. She stood still for a few seconds as though uncertain about leaving the security of the bushes, then curiosity got the better of her caution, and she stepped out.

I stared at her because she was completely a stranger. From time to time there were gatherings or parties which brought together all the children for miles around, so that it was astonishing to encounter one that I had never seen before.

"What's your name?" I asked her.

"Sophie," she told me. "What's yours?"

"David," I said. "Where's your home?"

"Over there," she said, waving her hand vaguely toward the foreign country beyond the bank.

Her eyes left mine and went to the sandy runnel down which I had been sliding.

"Is that fun?" she inquired, with a wistful look.

I hesitated a moment before inviting her. "Yes," I told her. "Come and try."

She hung back, studying me with a serious expression for a second or two, then made up her mind quite suddenly. She scrambled to the top of the bank ahead of me.

She sped down the runnel with curls and ribbons flying. When I landed she had lost her serious look, and her eyes were dancing with excitement.

"Again," she said, and panted back up the bank.

It was on her third descent that the misadventure occurred. She sat down and shoved off as before. I watched her swish down and come to a stop in a flurry of sand. Somehow she had contrived to land a couple of feet to the left of the usual place. I made ready to follow, and waited for her to get clear. She did not.

"Go on," I told her, impatiently.

She tried to move, and then called up, "I can't. It hurts."

I risked pushing off anyway, and landed close beside her.

"What's the matter?" I asked.

Her face was screwed up. Tears stood in her eyes. "My foot's stuck," she said.

Her left foot was buried. I scrabbled the soft sand clear with my hands. Her shoe was jammed in a narrow space between two up-pointed stones. I tried to move it, but it would not budge.

"Can't you sort of twist it out?" I suggested.

She tried, lips valiantly compressed.

"It won't come."

"I'll help pull," I offered.

"No, no! It hurts," she protested.

I did not know what to do next, but I was favorably impressed by her stoicism. All the other small girls I knew—and some of the boys, too—would have been yelling their heads off in the circumstances. Very clearly her predicament was painful. I considered the problem.

"We'd better cut the laces so you can pull your foot out of the shoe. I can't reach the knot," I decided.

"No!" she said, alarmedly. "No, I mustn't."

She was so emphatic that I was baffled. If she would pull her foot out of the shoe, we might knock the shoe itself free with a stone, but if she would not, I did not see what was to be done. She lay back on the sand, the knee of the trapped leg sticking up in the air.

"Oh, it is hurting so," she said. She could not hold back the tears any longer. They ran down her face. But even then she didn't howl. She made small puppyish noises.

"You'll *have* to take it off," I told her.

"No!" she protested again. "No. I mustn't. Not ever. I mustn't."

Whatever the reason for it, there was no mistaking her intensity. I sat down beside her, at a loss. Both her hands held on to one of mine, gripping it tightly while she cried. It was obvious that the pain of her foot was increasing. For almost the first time in my life I found myself in charge of a situation which demanded a decision. I made it.

"It's no good. You've *got* to get it off," I told her. "If you don't, you'll probably stay here and die."

She did not give in at once, but her argument weakened until at last she consented. She watched apprehensively while I cut the lace. Then she said:

"Go away! You mustn't look."

I hesitated, but childhood is a time thickly beset with incomprehensible, though important, conventions; I withdrew a few yards and turned my back. I heard her breathing hard. Then she was crying again. I turned around to help her.

"I can't do it," she said, looking at me fearfully through her tears. I knelt down to see what I could do about it.

"You mustn't ever tell," she said. "Never, *never*. Promise?"

I promised.

She was very brave about it. Nothing more than the puppy noises.

When I did succeed in getting the foot free, it looked queer; I mean, it was all twisted and puffy—I didn't even notice then that it had more than the usual number of toes. . . .

I managed to hammer the shoe out of the cleft, and handed it to her. But she found she could not put it on her swollen foot. Nor could she put the foot to the ground. I thought I might carry her on my back, but she was heavier than I expected, and it was clear that we should not get far that way.

"I'll have to go and fetch somebody to help," I told her.

"No. I'll crawl," she said.

I walked beside her, carrying the shoe, and feeling useless. She kept going gamely for a surprisingly long way, but she had to give it up. Her trousers were worn through at the knees, and the knees themselves were sore and bleeding. I had never known anyone, boy or girl, who would have kept on till that pitch; it awed me slightly. I helped her to stand up on her sound foot, and steadied her while she pointed out where her home was, and the trickle of smoke that marked it. I set off half-running, with a high sense of responsibility. When I looked back she was on all fours again, disappearing into the bushes.

I found the house without much difficulty, and knocked, a little nervously. A tall woman answered. She had a fine, handsome face with large bright eyes. Her dress was russet and a little shorter than those most of the women at home wore, but it carried the conventional cross, from neck to hem and breast to breast, in a green that matched the scarf on her head.

"Are you Sophie's mother?" I asked.

She looked at me sharply and frowned. She said, with anxious abruptness:

"What is it?"

I told her.

"Oh," she said. "Her foot!"

She looked hard at me again for a moment, then she stood the broom she was holding against the wall, and asked briskly:

"Where is she?"

I led her by the way I had come. At the sound of her voice Sophie crawled out of the bushes.

Her mother looked at the swollen, misshapen foot and the bleeding knees.

"Oh, my poor darling!" she said, holding her and kissing her. Then she added: "He's seen it?"

"Yes," Sophie told her. "I'm sorry, Mummy. I tried hard, but I couldn't do it myself, and it did hurt so."

Her mother nodded slowly. She sighed.

"Oh, well. It can't be helped now. Up you get."

Sophie climbed on to her mother's back, and we all went back to the house together.

The commandments and precepts one learns as a child are just a set of bits; parts of no pattern, few of them even touching one another. Some lodge and are remembered by rote, but they mean little until there is example—and, even then, the example needs to be recognized.

Thus, I was able to sit patiently and watch the hurt foot being washed, cold-poulticed, and bound up, and perceive no connection between it and the affirmation which I had heard almost every Sunday of my life. I could repeat the words of the affirmation, just as I could repeat many other sets of words, but it had simply never occurred to me that they had any connection with real life or real people. They were just something that got said on Sunday:

"And God created man in his own image. And God decreed that man should have one body, one head, two arms and two legs; that each arm should be jointed in two places and end in one hand; that each hand should have four fingers and one thumb; that each finger should bear a flat finger-nail . . ."

And so on until:

"Then God created woman, also, and in the same image, but with these differences, according to her nature: her voice should be of higher pitch than man's; she should grow no beard; she should have two breasts . . ."

And so on again.

I knew it all, word for word—and yet the sight of Sophie's six toes stirred nothing in my memory. They looked no less proper to her foot than my five did to my own. I saw the foot resting in her mother's lap. Watched her mother pause to look down at it for a still moment, lift it, bend to kiss it gently, and then look up with tears in her eyes. I felt sorry for her distress, and for Sophie, and for the hurt foot—but nothing more.

While the bandaging was being finished I looked around the room curiously. The house was a great deal smaller than my home, a cottage, in fact, but I liked it better. It felt friendly. And although Sophie's mother was anxious and worried she spoke to me now and then as if I was as real a person as herself. She did not give me the feeling that I was the one regrettable and unreliable factor in an otherwise orderly life, the way most people did at home. And the room itself seemed to me the better, too, for not having groups of words hanging on the wall that people could point to in disapproval. At home they had been doing that since long before I had been able to read the words. Instead, this room had several drawings of horses, which I thought very fine.

Presently, Sophie, tidied up now, and with the tearstains washed away, hopped to a chair at the table. Quite restored but for the foot, she inquired with grave hospitality whether I liked eggs.

I said I did.

Afterward, her mother told me to wait where I was while she carried Sophie upstairs. She returned in a few minutes, and sat down beside me. She took my hand in hers and looked at me seriously for some moments. I could feel her anxiety strongly; though quite why she should be so worried was not, at first, clear to me. I was surprised by her, for there had been no sign before that she could think in that way. I thought back to her, trying to reassure her and show her that she need not be anxious about me, but it didn't reach her. She went on looking at me with her eyes shining, much as Sophie's had when she was trying not to cry. Her thoughts were all worry and shapeless as she kept on looking at me, I tried again but still couldn't reach them. Then she nodded slowly, and said in words:

"You're a good boy, David. You were very kind to Sophie. I want to thank you for that."

I felt awkward, and looked at my shoes. I couldn't remember anyone saying before that I was a good boy. I knew no form of response designed to meet such an event.

"You like Sophie, don't you?" she went on, still looking at me.

"Yes," I told her. And I added: "I think she's awfully brave, too. It must have hurt a lot."

"Will you keep a secret—an important secret—for her sake?" she asked.

"Yes, of course," I agreed, but a little uncertain in my tone for not realizing what the secret was.

"You—you saw her foot?" she said, looking steadily into my face. "Her—toes?"

I nodded. "Yes," I said again.

"Well, that is the secret, David. Nobody else must know about that. You are the only person who does, except her father and me. Nobody else must know. Nobody at all—not ever."

"No," I agreed, and nodded seriously again.

There was a pause—at least, her voice paused, but her thoughts went on, as if "nobody" and "not ever" were making desolate, unhappy echoes there. Then that changed and she became tense and fierce and afraid inside. It was no good thinking back to her. I tried clumsily to emphasize in words that I had meant what I said.

"Never—not anybody at all," I assured her earnestly.

"It's very, very important," she insisted. "How can I explain to you?" But she didn't really need to explain. Her urgent, tight-strung feeling of the importance was very plain. Her words were far less potent. She said:

"If anyone were to find out, they'd—they'd be terribly unkind to her. We've got to see that that never happens."

It was as if the anxious feeling had turned into something hard, like an iron rod.

"Because she has six toes?" I asked.

"Yes. That's what nobody but us must ever know. It must be a secret between us," she repeated, driving it home. "You'll promise, David."

"I'll promise. I can swear, if you like," I offered.

"The promise is enough," she told me.

It was so heavy a promise that I was quite resolved to keep it completely—even from my cousin Rosalind. Though, underneath, I was puzzled by its evident importance. It seemed a very small toe to cause such a degree of anxiety. But there was a great deal of grown-up fuss that seemed disproportionate to causes. If I had not learned long ago that a grown-up could scarcely ever give a satisfactory answer to a simple question I would have asked her just *why* it was so important, and *why* anybody should be unkind to Sophie on account of it. But as one was liable sometimes to get punished simply for putting a question at all, I had got into the habit of not asking things much. So I held on to the main point—the need for secrecy. That would not be difficult. I could just tuck it in among my rather large range of private secrets, though it would be unusual to have one I could not share even with Rosalind.

Sophie's mother kept on looking at me with a sad, but unseeing expression until I became uncomfortable. She noticed as I fidgeted, and smiled. It was a kind smile.

"All right, then," she said. "We'll keep it secret, and never talk about it again?"

"Yes," I agreed.

On the way down the path from the door, I turned around.

"May I come and see Sophie again soon?" I asked.

She hesitated, giving the question some thought, then she said:

"Very well—if you are sure you can come without anyone knowing."

Not until I had reached the bank and was making my homeward way along the top of it did the monotonous Sunday precepts join up with reality. Then, suddenly, the Definition of Man recited itself in my head: "—and each leg shall be jointed twice and have one foot, and each foot five toes, and each toe shall end with a flat nail . . ." And so on, until finally: "And any creature that shall seem to be human, but is not formed thus is not human. It is neither man nor woman. It is a Blasphemy against the true Image of God, and hateful in the sight of God."

I was abruptly perturbed—and considerably puzzled, too. A Blasphemy was, as had been impressed upon me often enough, a frightful thing. Yet there was nothing frightful about Sophie. She was simply an ordinary little girl—if a great deal more sensible and braver than most. Yet, according to the Definition . . .

Clearly there must be a mistake somewhere. Surely having one very small toe extra—well, two very small toes, because I supposed there would be one to match on the other foot—surely that couldn't be enough to make one "hateful in the sight of God?"

The ways of the world were very puzzling. In the course of my ten years I had accumulated quite a lot of lore of one kind and another, bits from church, bits from my parents, bits from lessons, bits from other children, bits from adventuring on my own, but they were still disjointed and not to be relied upon for guidance. When I did something amiss, I still had little but the scale of the punishment to indicate whether I had committed an enormity, or a peccadillo. The things I knew did not connect to make a clear course of conduct. The best I could do was to cling to the simpler things that I did understand—things like a promise being a promise. That, at least, was clear and straightforward.

Chapter Two

I REACHED HOME by my usual method. At a point where the woods had lapped up the side of the bank and grown across it I scrambled down on to a narrow, little-used track. From there on I was watchful, and kept my hand on my knife. I was supposed to keep out of the woods, for it did occasionally—though very rarely—happen that large creatures penetrated as far into civilized parts as Waknuk, and there was just a chance that one might encounter some kind of wild dog or cat. However, and as usual, the only creatures I heard were small ones, hurriedly making off.

After a mile or so I reached cultivated land, with the house in sight across three or four fields. I worked along the fringe of the woods, observing carefully from cover, then crossed all but the last field in the shadows of the hedges, and paused to prospect again. There was no one in sight but old Jacob slowly shoveling muck in the yard. When his back was safely turned I cut swiftly across the bit of open ground, climbed in through a window, and made my way cautiously to my own room. One of the troubles about home was that if one walked in by a door there would almost certainly be some person who, after a what-have-you-been-up-to-now? question, would find one a useful, but uncongenial job.

Our house is not easy to describe. My grandfather, Elias Strorm, built the first part of it over fifty years before; since then it had grown new rooms and extensions at various times. By now, it rambled off on one side into stock-sheds, stores, stables, and barns, and on the other into washhouses, dairies, cheese-rooms, farmhands' rooms, and so on until it three-quarters enclosed a large, beaten-earth yard which lay to leeward of the main house and had a midden for its central feature.

Like all the houses of the district to which it had given its name, it was constructed on a frame of solid, roughly dressed timbers, but, since it was the oldest house there, most of the spaces in the outer walls had been filled in with bricks and stones from the ruins of some of the Old People's buildings, and plastered wattle was used only for the internal walls.

My grandfather, in the aspect he wore when presented to me by my father as an example, appeared to have been a man of somewhat tediously unrelieved virtue. It was only later that I pieced together a portrait that was more credible, if less creditable.

Elias Strorm came from the east, somewhere near the sea. Why he came is not quite clear. He himself maintained that it was the ungodly ways of the East which drove him to search for a less sophisticated, stauncher-minded region; though I have heard it suggested that there came a point when his native parts refused to tolerate him any longer. Whatever the cause, it persuaded him to Waknuk—then undeveloped, almost frontier country—with all his worldly goods in a train of six wagons, at the age of forty-five. He was a husky man, a dominating man, and a man fierce for rectitude. He had eyes that could flash with evangelical fire beneath bushy brows. Respect for God was frequently on his lips, and fear of the devil constantly in his heart, and it seems to have been hard to say which inspired him the more.

Soon after he had started the house he went off on a journey and brought back a bride. She was shy, pretty in the pink and golden way, and twenty-five years younger than himself. She moved, I have been told, like a lovely colt when she thought herself unwatched; as timorously as a rabbit when she felt her husband's eye upon her.

All her answers, poor thing, were dusty. She did not find that a marriage service generated love; she did not enable her husband to recapture his youth through hers; nor could she compensate for that by running his home in the manner of an experienced housekeeper.

Elias was not a man to let shortcomings pass unremarked. In a few seasons he straightened the coltishness with admonitions, faded the pink and gold with preaching, and produced a sad, gray wraith of wifehood who died, unprotesting, a year after her second son was born.

Grandfather Elias had never a moment's doubt of the proper pattern for his heir. My father's faith was bred into his bones, his principles were his sinews, and both responded to a mind richly stored with instances from the Bible, and from Nicholson's *Repentances*. In faith father and son were at one; the difference between them was only in approach; the evangelical flash did not appear in my father's eyes; his virtue was more legalistic.

Joseph Strorm, my father, did not marry until Elias was dead, and when he did, he was not a man to repeat his father's mistakes. My mother's views harmonized with his own. She had a strong sense of duty, and never doubted where it lay.

Our district, and, consequently, our house as the first there, took the name Waknuk because of a tradition that there had been a place of that name there, or thereabouts, long, long ago, in the time of the Old People. The tradition was, as usual, vague, but certainly there had been some buildings there, for remnants and foundations had remained until they were taken for new buildings. There was also the long bank, running away until it reached the hills and the huge scar there that must have been made by the Old People when, in their superhuman fashion, they had cut away half a mountain in order to find something or other that interested them. It may have been called Waknuk then; anyway, Waknuk it had become, an orderly, law-abiding, God-respecting community of some hundred scattered holdings, large and small.

My father was a man of local consequence. When, at the age of sixteen, he had made his first public appearance by giving a Sunday address in the church his father had built, there had still been fewer than sixty families in the district. But as more land was cleared for farming and more people came to settle, he was not submerged by them. He was still the largest landowner, he still continued to preach frequently on Sundays and explain with practical clarity the laws and views held in heaven upon a variety of matters and practices, and he continued upon the appointed days to administer the laws temporal, as a magistrate. For the rest of the time he saw to it that he, and all within his control, continued to set a high example to the district.

Within the house, life centered, as was the local custom, upon the large living room which was also the kitchen. As the house was the largest and best in Waknuk, so was the room. The great fireplace there was an object of pride—not vain pride, of course; more a matter of being conscious of having given worthy treatment to the excellent materials that the Lord had provided: a kind of testament, really. The hearth was solid stone blocks. The whole chimney was built of bricks and had never been known to catch fire. The area about its point of emergence was covered with the only tiles in the district, so that the thatch which covered the rest of the roof had never caught fire, either.

My mother saw to it that the big room was kept very clean and tidy. The floor was composed of pieces of brick and stone and artificial stone cleverly fitted together. The furniture was whitely scrubbed tables and stools, with a few chairs. The walls were whitewashed. Several burnished pans, too big to go in the cupboards, hung against them. The nearest approach to decoration was a number of wooden panels with sayings, mostly from *Repentances,* artistically burnt into them. The one on the left of the fireplace read: ONLY THE IMAGE OF GOD IS MAN. The one on the right: KEEP PURE THE STOCK OF THE LORD. On the opposite wall two more said: BLESSED IS THE NORM, and IN PURITY OUR SALVATION. The largest was the one on the back wall, hung to face the door which led to the yard. It reminded everyone who came in: WATCH THOU FOR THE MUTANT!

Frequent references to these texts had made me familiar with the words long before I was able to read; in fact I am not sure that they did not give me my first reading lessons. I knew them by heart, just as I knew others elsewhere in the house which said things like: THE NORM IS THE WILL OF GOD, and, REPRODUCTION IS THE ONLY HOLY PRODUCTION, and, THE DEVIL IS THE FATHER OF DEVIATION, and a number of others about Offenses and Blasphemies.

Many of them were still obscure to me; others I had learnt something about. Offenses, for instance. That was because the occurrence of an Offense was sometimes quite an impressive occasion. Usually the first sign that one had happened was that my father came into the house in a bad temper. Then, in the evening, he would call us all together, including everyone who worked on the farm. We would all kneel while he proclaimed our repentance and led prayers for forgiveness. The next morning we would all be up before daylight, and gather in the yard. As the sun rose we would sing a hymn while my father ceremonially slaughtered the two-headed calf, four-legged chicken, or whatever other kind of Offense it happened to be. Sometimes it would be a much queerer thing than those. The most exciting time I remember was when a goose proudly led her brood into the yard one day. She must somehow have reared them in the woods, for they were already the size of hens. Not only were they web-winged instead of feathered, but they also had exceedingly sharp beaks and vicious tempers. There was a very active scene in the yard before a much-pecked and scratched company assembled to ask a blessing on their liquidation.

But Offenses were not limited to the livestock. Sometimes it would be some stalks of corn, or some vegetables, that my father produced and cast on the kitchen table in anger and shame. If it was merely a matter of a few rows of vegetables, they just came out and were destroyed. But if a whole field had gone wrong we would wait for good weather, and then set fire to it, singing hymns while it burnt. I used to find that a very fine sight.

It was because my father was a careful and pious man with a keen eye for an Offense that we used to have more slaughterings and burnings than anyone else. Any suggestion that we were more afflicted with Offenses than other people hurt and angered him. He had no wish at all to throw good money away, he pointed out. If our neighbors were as conscientious as ourselves, he had no doubt that their liquidations would far outnumber ours; unfortunately there were certain persons with elastic principles.

So I learned quite early to know what Offenses were. They were things which did not look *right*—that is to say, did not look like their parents, or parent-plants. Usually there was only some small thing wrong—though sometimes a thing might have gone altogether wrong, and be very queer indeed.

But however much or little was wrong it was on Offense, and if it happened among people it was a Blasphemy—at least, that was the technical term though commonly both kinds were called Deviations.

Nevertheless, the question of Offenses was not always as simple as one might think. When there was disagreement the district's Inspector would be sent for. He would examine the dubious creature or plant carefully, and more often than not he would decide it was an Offense—but sometimes he would proclaim it simply a Cross. In that case it was usually allowed to survive although nobody thought much of Crosses. My father, however, seldom called in the Inspector, he preferred to be on the safe side and liquidate anything doubtful. There were people who disapproved of his meticulousness, saying that the local Deviation-rate, which had shown a steady over-all improvement and now stood at half what it had been in my grandfather's time, would have been better still but for my father. Nevertheless, the Waknuk district had a great name for Purity.

Ours was no longer a frontier region. Hard work and sacrifice had produced a stability of stock and crops which could be envied even by some communities to the east of us. You could now go some thirty miles to the south or southwest before you came to Wild Country—that is to say parts where the chance of breeding true was less than fifty per cent. After that, everything grew more erratic across a belt which was ten miles wide in some places and up to twenty in others, until you came to the mysterious Fringes where nothing was dependable, and where, to quote my father, "the Devil struts his wide estates, and the laws of God are mocked." Fringes country, too, was said to be variable in depth, and beyond it lay the Badlands about which nobody knew anything. Usually anybody who went into the Badlands died there, and the one or two men who had come out of them did not last long.

It was not the Badlands, but the Fringes that gave us trouble from time to time. The people of the Fringes—at least, one calls them people, because although they were really Deviations they often looked quite like ordinary human people, if nothing had gone too much wrong with them—these people, then, had very little where they lived in their border country, so they came out into civilized parts to steal grain and livestock and clothes and tools and weapons, too, if they could; and sometimes they carried off children.

Occasional small raids used to happen two or three times a year, and nobody took much notice of them as a rule—except the people who got raided, of course. Usually they had time to get away and lost only their stock. Then everybody would contribute a little in kind, or in money, to help them set up again. But as time went on and the frontier was pushed back there were more Fringes people trying to live on less country. Some years they got very hungry, and after a time it was no longer just a matter of a dozen or so making a quick raid and then running back into Fringes country; they came instead in large, organized bands and did a lot of damage.

In my father's childhood mothers used to quieten and awe troublesome infants by threatening, "Be good now. Or I'll fetch Old Maggie from the Fringes to you. She's got four eyes to watch you with, and four ears to hear you with, and four arms to smack you with. So you be careful." Or Hairy Jack was another ominous figure who might be called in. ". . . and he'll take you off to his cave in the Fringes where all his family lives. They're all hairy, too, with long tails; and they eat a little boy each for breakfast every morning, and a little girl each for supper every evening." Nowadays, however, it was not only small children who lived in nervous awareness of the Fringes people not so far away. Their existence had become a dangerous nuisance and their depredations the cause of many representations to the government in Rigo.

For all the good the petitions did, they might never have been sent. Indeed, with no one able to tell, over a stretch of five or six hundred miles, where the next attack would come, it is difficult to see what practical help could have been given. What the government did do, from its comfortable situation far, far to the east, was to express sympathy in encouraging phrases, and suggest the formation of a local militia—a suggestion which, as all able-bodied males had as a matter of course been members of a kind of unofficial militia since frontier days, was felt to amount to disregard of the situation.

As far as the Waknuk district was concerned the threat from the Fringes was more of a nuisance than a menace. The deepest raid had come no nearer than ten miles, but every now and then there were emergencies, and seemingly more every year, which called the men away, and brought all the farm work to a stop. The interruptions were expensive and wasteful; moreover, they always brought anxiety if the trouble was near our sector: nobody could be sure that they might not come further one time. . . .

Mostly, however, we led a comfortable, settled, industrious existence. Our household was extensive. There were my father and mother, my two sisters, and my Uncle Axel to make the family, but also there were the kitchen girls and dairymaids, some of whom were married to the farm men, and their children, and, of course, the men themselves, so when we were all gathered for the meal at the end of the day's work there were over twenty of us; and when we assembled for prayers there were still more because the men from the adjoining cottages came in with their wives and children.

Uncle Axel was not a real relative. He had married one of my mother's sisters, Elizabeth. He was a sailor then, and she had gone east with him and died in Rigo while he was on the voyage that had left him a cripple. He was a useful all-around man, though slow in getting about because of his leg, so my father let him live with us. He was also my best friend.

My mother came of a family of five girls and two boys. Four of the girls were full sisters; the youngest girl and the two boys were half-sister and half-brothers to the rest. Hannah, the eldest, had been sent away by her husband, and nobody had heard of her since. Emily, my mother, was next in age. Then came Harriet, who was married to a man with a big farm at Kentak, almost fifteen miles away. Then Elizabeth, who had married Uncle Axel. Where my half-aunt Lilian and my half-uncle Thomas were I did not know, but my half-uncle Angus Morton owned the farm next to us, and a mile or more of our boundaries ran together, which annoyed my father, who could scarcely agree with half-uncle Angus about anything. His daughter, Rosalind, was, of course, my cousin.

Although Waknuk itself was the biggest farm in the district, most of them were organized along the same lines, and all of them growing larger, for with the improving stability-rate there was the incentive to extend; every year felling of trees and clearing went on to make new fields. The woods and spurs of forest were being nibbled away until the country-side was beginning to look like the old, long-cultivated land in the east.

It was said that nowadays even people in Rigo knew where Waknuk was without looking it up on the map.

I lived, in fact, on the most prosperous farm in a prospering district. At the age of ten, however, I had little appreciation of that. My impression was of an uncomfortably industrious place where there always seemed to be more jobs than people, unless one was careful, so on this particular evening I contrived to lie low until routine sounds told me that it was near enough to the mealtime for me to show myself safely.

As I wandered into the yard I encountered Janet, bringing in a big jug of milk from the dairy. She looked at me suspiciously.

"And where've you been?" she inquired. "Your father was wanting you to give the pony some exercise."

I was ready for that. "Fishing," I told her, unblushingly, "Down below the mill."

I hung about, watching the horses being unharnessed and turned out. Presently the bell on the gable-end tolled a couple of times. Doors opened, and people came into the yard, making for the kitchen. I went along with them. The warning: WATCH THOU FOR THE MUTANT! faced me as I went in, but it was much too familiar to stir a thought. What interested me exclusively at the moment was the smell of food.

Chapter Three

I USUALLY WENT OVER to see Sophie once or twice a week after that. What schooling we had—which was a matter of half a dozen children being taught to read and write and do some sums by one or another of several old women—took place in the mornings. It was not difficult at the midday meal to slip away from the table early and disappear until everyone would think someone else had found a job for me, but I felt it would be unwise to do that too often, and made a point of letting someone find work for me two or three afternoons a week.

Very often I did not need to go all the way to Sophie's home to find her. Sometimes I'd hear her call, but see no sign of her until she came pushing out of the bushes, or popping up from behind a tuft of grass.

When her ankle was quite recovered she was able to show me the favorite corners of her territory. Most often we went to the stream. She liked to watch the fish in the pools there. In order not to disturb them we'd crawl to the bank and push our heads over very slowly and carefully. There were some queer things to be seen sometimes.

One day we were watching a fish with a dark line on its back that broke into speckles on its sides. It hung suspended, facing upstream, opening its mouth in a leisurely way now and then to gulp morsels that were washed toward it. Sophie nudged me. I followed her line of sight, and saw a larger fish, lurking beneath an overhanging bush like a long shadow. It was watching the midstream fish attentively, and for all its present lack of motion it looked tense and ready to pounce, but beneath and behind it was something else again. A creature on long, stilty legs with sharp-looking claws wide, and reaching forward. Its tail was curled under it and fanning very gently as it crept closer and closer to the intent larger fish.

We watched, fascinated. The drama was painfully prolonged. Still the larger fish awaited the perfect moment, while the other creature inched delicately nearer to it.

Suddenly Sophie shouted "No!" and threw a stone. When the ripples cleared the tableau had vanished.

"What did you do that for?" I said. I had wanted to see how it would work out.

"The horrible thing was going to get him. They nearly always do."

"Are there a lot of them in there?" I asked, looking down into the water.

"Oh, yes. My father catches them sometimes. They're nice to eat, although they're horrible."

"It looked like an Offense," I said. "You ought to burn Offenses, not eat them."

"Why?"

I was not sure about that, but I knew it was the proper thing to do. I told her that we always did it at home.

"But that's silly if they're good to eat," she decided.

It was, I explained, a matter of principle. I did not know quite what that meant, either, but I was sure it was what my father would have said in the circumstances.

"Oh," said Sophie, vaguely, but she looked a little impressed, all the same.

One day I took her over our side of the big bank to see the steam-engine. There wasn't another steam-engine within a hundred miles, and we were very proud of it. Corky, who looked after it, was not about, but the doors at the end of its shed were open, letting out the sound of a rythmic groaning, creaking, and puffing. We ventured onto the threshold and peered into the gloom inside. It was fascinating to watch the big timbers moving up and down with wheezing noises while up in the shadows of the roof a huge crossbeam rocked slowly backward and forward, with a pause at the end of each tilt as though it were summoning up energy for the next effort. Fascinating—but, after a time, monotonous.

Ten minutes of it were enough, and we withdrew to climb to the top of the woodpile beside the shed. We sat there with the whole heap quivering beneath us as the engine chugged ponderously on.

"My Uncle Axel says the Old People must have had much better engines than this," I told her.

"My father says that if one-quarter of the things they say about the Old People are true, they must have been magicians, not real people, at all," Sophie countered.

"But they *were* wonderful," I insisted.

"Too wonderful to be true, he says," she told me.

"Doesn't he think they were able to fly, like people say?" I asked.

"No. That's silly. If they could've, we'd be able to."

"But there are lots of things they could do that we are learning to do again," I protested.

"Not flying," she shook her head. "Things can either fly, or they can't; and we can't," she said.

I thought of telling her about my dream of the city and the things flying over it, but after all, a dream isn't much evidence of anything, so I let it pass. Presently we climbed down, leaving the engine to its panting and creaking and made our way over to her home.

John Wender, her father, was back from one of his trips. A sound of hammering came from the outside shed where he was stretching skins on frames, and the whole place smelled of his operations. Sophie rushed to him and flung her arms round his neck. He straightened up, holding her against him with one arm.

"Hullo, Chicky," he said.

He greeted me more gravely. We had an unspoken understanding that we were on a man-to-man basis. It had not always been like that. When he first saw me he had looked at me in a way that had scared me and made me afraid to speak in his presence. Gradually, however, that had changed. We became friends. He showed me and told me a lot of interesting things—all the same I would look up sometimes to find him watching me uneasily.

And no wonder. Only some years later could I appreciate how badly troubled he must have been when he came home to find Sophie had sprained her ankle, and that it had been David Strorm, the son of Joseph Strorm, of all people, who had seen her foot. He must, I think, have been greatly tempted by the thought that a dead boy could break no promise. It would have been understandable. Perhaps Mrs. Wender saved me.

But I think he would have been reassured had he known of an incident at my home about a month after I met Sophie.

I had run a splinter into my hand and when I pulled it out it bled a lot. I went to the kitchen with it only to find everybody too busy getting supper to be bothered with me, so I rummaged a strip out of the rag-drawer for myself. I tried clumsily for a minute or two to tie it, then my mother noticed. She made tchk-tchk noises of disapproval and insisted on it being washed. Then she wound the strip on neatly, grumbling that of course I must go and do it just when she was busy. I said I was sorry, and added:

"I could have managed it all right by myself if I'd had another hand."

My voice must have carried, for silence fell on the whole room like a clap.

My mother froze. I looked around the room at the sudden quiet. Mary, standing with a pie in her hands, two of the four men waiting for their meal, my father about to take his seat at the head of the table, and the others; they were all staring at me. I caught my father's expression just as it was turning from amazement to anger. Alarmed, but uncomprehending, I watched his mouth tighten, his jaw come forward, his brows press together over his still-incredulous eyes. He demanded:

"What was that you said, boy?"

I knew the tone. I tried to think in a desperate hurry how I had offended this time. I stumbled and stuttered.

"I—I s-said I couldn't manage to tie this for myself," I told him.

His eyes had become less incredulous, more accusing.

"And you wished you had a third hand!"

"No, father. I only said *if* I had another hand——"

"——you would be able to tie it. If that was not a wish, what was it?"

"I only meant *if*," I protested. I was alarmed, and too confused to explain that I had only happened to use one way of expressing a difficulty which might have been put in several ways. I was aware that the rest had stopped gaping at me, and were now looking apprehensively at my father. His expression was grim.

"You—my own son—were calling upon the Devil to give you another hand!" he accused me.

"But I wasn't. I only——"

"Be quiet, boy. Everyone in this room heard you. You'll certainly make it no better by lying."

"But——"

"Were you, or were you not, expressing dissatisfaction with the form of the body God gave you—the form in his own image?"

"I just said *if* I——"

"You blasphemed, boy. You found fault with the Norm. Everybody here heard you. What have you to say to that? You know what the Norm is?"

I gave up protesting. I knew well enough that my father in his present mood would not try to understand. I muttered, parrot-like:

" 'The Norm is the Image of God.' "

"You *do* know. And yet, knowing this, you deliberately wished yourself a Mutant. That is a terrible thing, an outrageous thing. You, my son, committing blasphemy before his parents!" In his sternest pulpit voice, he added: "What is a Mutant?"

" 'A thing accursed in the sight of God and man,' " I mumbled.

"And *that* is what you wished to be! What have you to say?"

With a heart-sunk certainty that it would do useless to say anything I kept my lips shut and my eyes lowered.

"Down on your knees!" he commanded. "Kneel and pray!"

The others all knelt, too. My father's voice rose:

"Lord, we have sinned in omission. We beg thy forgiveness that we have not better instructed this child in thy laws. . . ." The prayer seemed to go booming on for a long time. After the "Amen" there was a pause, until my father said:

"Now go to your room and pray. Pray, you wretched boy, for a forgiveness you do not deserve, but which God, in his mercy, may yet grant you. I will come to you later."

I went to my room, but I did not pray. I sat miserably on

the side of my bed while a feeling of bewildered shame gave way slowly to a feeling of injustice that glowed in my chest like a hot coal.

In the night, when the anguish which had followed my father's visit was somewhat abated, I lay awake, puzzling. I had had no idea of wishing for a third hand, but even if I had. . . . ? If it was such a terrible thing just to think of having three hands, what would happen if one really had them—or anything else wrong; such as, for instance, an extra toe. . . . ?

And when at last I fell asleep I had a dream.

We were all gathered in the yard, just as we had been at the last Purification. Then it had been a little hairless calf that stood waiting, blinking stupidly at the knife in my father's hand; this time it was a little girl, Sophie, standing barefooted and trying uselessly to hide the whole long row of toes that everyone could see on each foot. We all stood looking at her, and waiting. Presently she started to run from one person to another, imploring them to help her, but none of them moved, and none of their faces had any expression. My father started to walk toward her, the knife shining in his hand. Sophie grew frantic; she flitted from one unmoving person to another, tears running down her face. My father, stern, implacable, kept on coming nearer; still no one would move to help her. My father came closer still, with long arms outspread to prevent her bolting as he cornered her.

He caught her, and dragged her back to the middle of the yard. The sun's edge began to show above the horizon, and everyone started to sing a hymn. My father held Sophie with one arm just as he had held the struggling calf. He raised his other hand high, and as he swept it down the knife flashed in the light of the rising sun, just as it had flashed when he cut the calf's throat. . . .

If John and Mary Wender had been there when I woke up struggling and crying, and then lay in the dark trying to convince myself that the terrible picture which still hung in my mind was nothing more than a dream, they would, I think, have felt quite a lot easier in their minds.

Chapter Four

THIS WAS A TIME when I passed out of a placid period into one where things kept on happening. There wasn't much reason about it; that is to say, only a few of the things were connected with one another. It was more as if an active cycle had set in, just as a spell of different weather might come along.

My meeting with Sophie was, I suppose, the first incident; the next was that Uncle Axel found out about me and my half-cousin, Rosalind Morton. He—and it was lucky it was he, and no one else—happened to come upon me when I was talking to her, and I was doing it out loud because, although that way was slower, I could still be a lot clearer when I did it like that.

It must have been a self-preservative instinct which had made us keep the thing to ourselves, for we'd no active feeling of danger—I had so little, in fact, that when Uncle Axel found me sitting behind a rick chatting aparently to myself, I made very little effort to dissemble. He may have been there a minute or more before I became aware of somebody just around the corner of my eye, and turned to see who it was.

My Uncle Axel was a tall man, neither thin nor fat, but sturdy, and with a seasoned look to him. I used to think when I watched him at work that his weathered hands and forearms had some sort of kinship with the polished wood of the helves they used. He was standing in his customary way, with much of his weight upon the thick stick he used because his leg had been wrongly set when it was broken at sea. His bushy eyebrows, a a little touched with gray, were drawn closer by a half-frown, but the lines on his tanned face were half-amused as he regarded me.

"Well, Davie boy, and who would you be chattering away

so hard to? Is it fairies, or gnomes, or only the rabbits?" he asked.

I just shook my head. He limped closer, and sat down beside me, chewing on a stalk of grass from the rick.

"Feeling lonely?" he inquired.

"No," I told him.

He frowned a bit again. "Wouldn't it be more fun to do your chatting with some of the other kids?" he suggested. "More interesting than just sitting and talking to yourself?"

I hesitated, and then because he was Uncle Axel and my best friend among the grown-ups I said:

"But I was."

"Was what?" he asked, puzzled.

"Talking to one of them," I told him.

He frowned, and went on looking puzzled.

"Who?"

"Rosalind," I told him.

He paused a bit, looking at me harder.

"H'mm—I didn't see her around," he remarked.

"Oh, she isn't here. She's at home—at least, she's near home, in a little secret tree-house her brothers built in the woods," I explained. "It's a favorite place of hers."

He was not able to understand what I meant at first. He kept on talking as though it were a make-believe game; but after I had tried for some time to explain he sat quite quiet, watching my face as I talked, and presently his expression became very serious. After I'd stopped he said nothing, for a minute or two, then he asked:

"This isn't play-stuff, it's the real truth you're telling me, Davie boy?" And he looked at me hard and steadily as he spoke.

"Yes, Uncle Axel, of course," I assured him.

"And you've never told anyone else—nobody at all?"

"No. It's a secret," I told him, and he looked relieved.

He threw away the remains of his grass-stalk, and pulled another out of the rick. After he had thoughtfully bitten a few pieces off that and spat them out he looked directly at me again.

"Davie," he said, "I want you to make me a promise."

"Yes, Uncle Axel?"

"It's this," he said, speaking very seriously. "I want you to *keep* it secret. I want you to promise that you will never, never tell anyone else what you have just told me—*never*. It's very important; later on you'll understand better how important it is. You mustn't do anything that would even let anyone guess about it. Will you promise me that?"

His gravity impressed me greatly. I had never known him to speak with so much intensity. It made me aware, when I gave my promise, that I was vowing something more important than I could understand. He kept his eyes on mine as I spoke, and then nodded, satisfied that I meant it. We shook hands on the agreement. Then he said:

"It would be best if you could forget it altogether."

I thought it over, and then shook my head.

"I don't think I could do that, Uncle Axel. Not really. I mean, it just *is*. It'd be like trying to forget——" I broke off, unable to express what I wanted to.

"Like trying to forget how to talk, or how to hear, perhaps?" he suggested.

"Rather like that—only different," I admitted.

He nodded, and thought again.

"You hear the words inside your head?" he asked.

"Well not exactly 'hear,' and not exactly 'see,' " I told him. "There are—well, sort of shapes—and if you use words you make them clearer so that they're easier to understand."

"But you don't *have* to use words—not say them out loud as you were doing just now?"

"Oh no, it just helps to make it clearer sometimes."

"It also helps to make things a lot more dangerous, for both of you. I want you to make another promise: that you'll never do it out loud any more."

"All right, Uncle Axel," I agreed again.

"You'll understand when you're older how important it is," he told me, and then he went on to insist that I should get Rosalind to make the same promises. I did not tell him anything about the others because he seemed so worried already, but I decided I'd get them to promise, too. At the end he put out his hand again, and once more we swore secrecy very solemnly.

I put the matter to Rosalind and the others the same evening. It crystallized a feeling that was in all of us. I don't suppose that there was a single one of us who had not at some time made a slip or two and brought upon himself, or herself, an odd, suspicious look. A few of these looks had been warnings enough to each; it was such looks, not comprehended, but clear enough as signs of disapproval just below the verge of suspicion, that had kept us out of trouble. There had been no acknowledged, cooperative policy among us. It was simply as individuals that we had all taken the same self-protective, secretive course. But now, out of Uncle Axel's anxious insistence on my promise, the feeling of a threat was strengthened. It was still shapeless to us, but it was more real. Furthermore, in trying to convey Uncle Axel's seriousness to them I must have stirred up an uneasiness that was in all their minds, for there was no dissent. They made the promise willingly, eagerly, in fact, as thoug it was a burden they were relieved to share. It was our first act as a group; it *made* us a group by its formal admission of our responsibilities toward one another. It changed our lives by marking our first step in corporate self-preservation, though we understood little of that at the time. What seemed most important just then was the feeling of sharing.

Then, almost on top of that personal event came another which was of general concern; an invasion in force from the Fringes.

As usual, there was no detailed plan to deal with it. As near as anyone came to organization was the appointment of headquarters in the different sectors. Upon an alarm it was the duty of all able-bodied men in the district to rally at their local headquarters, when a course of action would be decided according to the location and extent of the trouble. As a method of dealing with small raids it had proved good enough, but that was all it was intended for. As a result, when the Fringes people found leaders who could promote an organized invasion there had been no adequately organized system of defense to delay them. They were able to push forward on a broad front, mopping up little bands of our militia here and there, looting as they liked and meeting nothing to delay them seriously until they were twenty-five miles or more into civilized parts.

By that time we had our forces in somewhat better order, and neighboring districts had pulled themselves together to head off a further widening, and harry the flanks. Our men were better-armed, too. Quite a lot of them had guns, whereas the Fringes people had only a few that they had stolen, and depended chiefly on bows, knives, and spears. Nevertheless, the width of their advance made them difficult to deal with. They were better woodsmen and cleverer at hiding themselves than proper human beings, so that they were able to press on another fifteen miles before we could contain them and bring them to battle.

It was exciting for a boy. With the Fringes people little more than seven miles away, our yard at Waknuk had become one of the rallying points. My father who had had an arrow through his arm early in the campaign, was helping to organize the new volunteers into squads. For several days there was a great bustling and coming and going as men were registered and sorted, and finally rode off with a fine air of determination and all the women of the household waving handkerchiefs at them.

When they had all departed, and our workers, too, the place seemed uncannily quiet for a day. Then there came a single rider, dashing back. He paused long enough to tell us that there had been a big battle and the Fringes people, with some of their leaders taken prisoner, were running away as fast as they could, then he galloped on with his good news.

That same afternoon a small troup of horsemen came riding into the yard, with two of the captured Fringes leaders in the middle of them.

I dropped what I was doing, and ran across to see. It was a bit disappointing at first sight. The tales about the Fringes had led me to expect creatures with two heads, or fur all over, or half a dozen arms and legs. Instead, they seemed at first glance to be just two ordinary men with beards—though unusually dirty, and with very ragged clothes. One of them was a short man with fair hair which was tufted as though he had trimmed it with a knife. But when I looked at the other I had a shock which brought me up dumbfounded, and staring at him. I was so jolted I just went on staring at him, for, put him in decent clothes, tidy up his beard, and he'd be the image of my father.

As he sat his horse, looking round, he noticed me; casually at first, in passing, then his gaze switched back and he stared hard at me. A strange look that I did not understand at all came into his eyes.

He opened his mouth as if to speak, but at that moment people came out of the house—my father, with his arm still in a sling, among them—to see what was going on.

I saw my father pause on the step and survey the group of horsemen, then he, too, noticed the man in the middle of them. For a moment he stood staring, just as I had done; then all his color drained away, and his face went blotchy gray.

I looked quickly at the other man. He was sitting absolutely rigid on his horse. The expression on his face made something clutch suddenly in my chest. I had never seen hatred naked before, the lines cut deep, the eyes glittering, the teeth suddenly looking like a savage animal's. It struck me with a slap, a horrid revelation of something hitherto unknown, and hideous; it stamped itself on my mind so that I never forgot it.

Then my father, still looking as though he was ill, put out his good hand to steady himself against the doorpost, and turned back into the house.

One of the escort cut the rope which held the prisoner's arms. He dismounted, and I was able to see then what was wrong with him. He stood some eighteen inches taller than anyone else, but not because he was a big man. If his legs had been right, he would have stood no taller than my father's five-foot-ten, but they were not; they were monstrously long and thin, and his arms were long and thin, too. It made him look half-man, half-spider.

The escort gave him food and a pot of beer. He sat down on a bench, and his bony knees stuck up to seem almost level with his shoulders. He looked around the yard, noticing everything as he munched his bread and cheese. In the course of his inspection he perceived me again. He beckoned. I hung back, pretending not to see. He beckoned again. I became ashamed of being afraid of him. I went closer, and then a little closer still, but keeping warily out of range, I judged, of those spidery arms.

"What's your name, boy?" he asked.

"David," I told him. "David Strorm."

He nodded, as though that was satisfactory.

"The man at the door, with his arm in a sling, that would be your father, Joseph Strorm?"

"Yes," I told him.

Again he nodded. He looked around the house and the outbuildings.

"This place, then, would be Waknuk?" he asked.

"Yes," I said again.

I don't know whether he would have asked more, for at that point somebody told me to clear off. A little later they all remounted, and soon they moved away, the spidery man with his arms tied together once more. I watched them ride off in the Kentak direction, glad to see them go. My first encounter with someone from the Fringes had not, after all, been exciting; it had been unpleasantly disturbing.

I heard later that both the captured Fringes men managed to escape that same night. I can't remember who told me, but I am perfectly certain it was not my father. I never once heard him refer to that day, and I never had the courage to question him about it.

Then scarcely, it seemed, had we settled down after the invasion and got the men back to catching up with the farm work, than my father was in the middle of a new row with my half-uncle, Angus Morton.

Differences of temperament and outlook had kept them intermittently at war with each other for years. My father had been heard to sum up his opinion by declaring that if Angus had any principles they were of such infinite width as to be a menace to the rectitude of the neighborhood; to which Angus was reputed to have replied that Joseph Strorm was a flinty-souled pedant, and bigoted well beyond the brink of stupidity. It was not, therefore, difficult for a row to blow up, and the latest one occurred over Angus's acquisition of a pair of greathorses.

Rumors of greathorses had reached our district though none had been seen there. My father was already uneasy in his mind at what he had heard of them, nor was the fact that it was Angus who had imported them a recommendation; consequently, it may have been with some prejudice that he went to inspect them.

His doubts were confirmed at once. The moment he set eyes on the huge creatures standing twenty-six hands at the shoulder, he knew they were *wrong*. He turned his back on them with disgust, and went straight to the Inspector's house with a demand that they should be destroyed as Offenses.

"You're out of order this time," the Inspector told him cheerfully, glad for once that his position was incontestable. "They're government-approved, so they are beyond my jurisdiction anyway."

"I don't believe it," my father told him. "God never made horses the size of these. The government *can't* have approved them."

"But they have," said the Inspector. "What's more," he added, with satisfaction, "Angus tells me that knowing the neighborhood so well he has got attested pedigrees for them."

"Any government that could pass creatures like that is corrupt and immoral," my father announced.

"Possibly," admitted the Inspector, "but it's still the government."

My father glared at him. "It's easy to see *why* some people would approve them," he said. "One of those brutes could do the work of two, maybe three, ordinary horses—and for less than double the feed of one. There's a good profit there, a good incentive to get them passed. But that doesn't mean that they're *right*. I say a horse like that is not one of God's creatures—and if it isn't his, then it's an Offense, and should be destroyed as such."

"The official approval states that the breed was produced simply by mating for size, in the normal way. And I'd defy you to find any characteristic that's identifiably wrong with them, anyway," the Inspector told him.

"It does not follow that they are *right*," my father persisted. "A horse that size is *not* right—you know that unofficially as well as I do, and there's no getting away from it. Once we allow things that we know are not right, there's no telling where it will end. A God-fearing community doesn't have to deny its faith just because there's been pressure brought to bear in a government licensing office. There are plenty of us here who know how God intended his creatures to be, even if the government doesn't."

The Inspector smiled. "As with the Dakerses' cat?" he suggested.

My father glared at him. The affair of the Dakerses' cat rankled.

About a year previously it had somehow come to his knowledge that Ben Dakers's wife housed a tailless cat. He investigated, and when he had collected evidence that it had not simply lost its tail in some way, but had never possessed one, he condemned it, and in his capacity as a magistrate ordered the Inspector to make out a warrant for its destruction as an Offense. The Inspector had done so, with reluctance, whereupon Dakers promptly entered an appeal. Such shilly-shallying in an obvious case outraged my father's principles, and he personally attended to the demise of the Dakerses' cat while the matter was still *sub judice*. His position, when a notification subsequently arrived stating that there was a recognized breed of tailless cats with a well-authenticated history, was awkward, and somewhat expensive. It had been with very bad grace that he had chosen to make a public apology rather than resign his magistracy.

"This," he told the Inspector sharply, "is an altogether more important affair."

"Listen," said the Inspector patiently. "The type is approved. This particular pair has confirmatory sanction. If that's not good enough for you, go ahead and shoot them yourself—and see what happens to you."

"It is your moral duty to issue an order against these so-called horses," my father insisted.

The Inspector was suddenly tired of it.

"It's part of my official duty to protect them from harm by fools or bigots," he snapped.

My father did not actually hit the Inspector, but it must have been a near thing. He went on boiling with rage for several days and the next Sunday we were treated to a searing address on the toleration of Mutants which sullied the Purity of our community. He called for a general boycott of the owner of the Offenses, speculated upon immorality in high places, hinted that some there might be expected to have a fellow-feeling for Mutants, and wound up with a peroration in which a certain official was scathed as an unprincipled hireling of unprincipled masters and the local representative of the Forces of Evil.

Though the Inspector had no such convenient pulpit for reply, certain trenchant remarks of his on persecution, contempt of authority, bigotry, religious mania, the law of slander, and the probable effects of direct action in opposition to government sanction achieved a wide circulation.

It was very likely the last point that kept my father from doing more than talk. He had had plenty of trouble over the Dakerses' cat which was of no value at all: but the great horses were costly creatures; besides, Angus would not be one to waive any possible penalty.

So there was a degree of frustration about that made home a good place to get away from as much as possible.

Now that the countryside had settled down again and was not full of unexpected people, Sophie's parents would let her go out on rambles once more, and I slipped away over there when I could get away unnoticed.

Sophie couldn't go to school, of course. She would have been found out very quickly, even with a false certificate, and her parents though they taught her to read and write did not have any books for her to read, so that it wasn't much good to her. That was why we talked —at least I talked—a lot on our expeditions, trying to tell her what I was learning from my reading books.

The world, I was able to tell her, was generally thought to be a pretty big place, and probably round. The civilized part of it, of which Waknuk was only a small district, was called Labrador. This was thought to be the Old People's name for it, though that was not very certain. Round most of Labrador there was a great deal of water called the sea, which was important on account of fish. Nobody that I knew, except Uncle Axel, had actually seen this sea because it was a long way off, but if you were to go three hundred miles or so east, north, or northwest you would come to it sooner or later. But southwest or south, you wouldn't; you'd get to the Fringes and then the Badlands, which would kill you.

It was said, too, though nobody was sure, that in the time of the Old People Labrador had been a cold land, so cold that no one could live there for long, so they had used it then only for growing trees and for their mysterious mining. But that had been a long, long time ago. A thousand years? Two thousand years? Even more, perhaps? People guessed, but nobody really knew. There was no telling how many generations of people had passed their lives like savages between the coming of Tribulation and the start of recorded history. Only Nicholson's *Repentances* had come out of the wilderness of barbarism, and that only because it had lain for, perhaps, several centuries sealed in a stone coffer before it was discovered. And only the Bible had survived from the time of the Old People themselves.

Except for what these two books told, the past, further back than three recorded centuries, was a long oblivion. Out of that blankness stretched a few strands of legend, badly frayed in their passage through successive minds. It was this long line of tongues that had given us the name Labrador, for it was unmentioned in either the Bible or *Repentances,* and they may have been right about the cold, although there were only two cold months in the year now; Tribulation could account for that, it could account for almost anything.

For a long time it had been disputed whether any parts of the world other than Labrador and the big island of Newf were populated at all. They were thought to be all Badlands which had suffered the full weight of Tribulation, but it had been found that there were some stretches of Fringes country in places. They were grossly deviational and quite godless, of course, and incapable of being civilized at present, but if the Badland borders were withdrawing there as ours were, it might one day be possible to colonize them.

Altogether, not much seemed to be known about the world, but at least it was a more interesting subject than Ethics, which an old man taught to a class of us on Sunday afternoons. Ethics was why you should, and shouldn't do things. Most of the don'ts were the same as my father's, but some of the reasons were different, so it was confusing.

According to Ethics, mankind—that was us, in civilized parts—was in the process of climbing back into grace; we were following a faint and difficult trail which led up to the peaks from which we had fallen. From the true trail branched many false trails that sometimes looked easier and more attractive; all these really led to the edges of precipices, beneath which lay the abyss of eternity. There was only one true trail, and by following it we should, with God's help and in his own good time, regain all that had been lost. But so faint was the trail, so set with traps and deceits, that every step must be taken with caution, and it was too dangerous for a man to rely on his own judgment. Only the authorities, ecclesiastical and lay, were in a position to judge whether the next step was a re-discovery, and so, safe to take; or whether it deviated from the true re-ascent, and so was sinful.

The penance of Tribulation that had been put upon the world must be worked out, the long climb faithfully retraced, and, at last, if the temptations by the way were resisted, there would be the reward of forgiveness—the restoration of the Golden Age. Such penances had been sent before: the expulsion from Eden, the Flood, pestilences, the destruction of the Cities of the Plain, the Captivity. Tribulation had been another such punishment, but the greatest of all. It must, when it struck have been not unlike a combination of all these disasters with something else, too, which caused a desolation far more frightful than flood and fire. Why it had been sent was as yet unrevealed, but, judging by precedent, there had very likely been a phase of irreligious arrogance prevailing at the time.

Most of the numerous precepts, arguments, and examples in Ethics were condensed for us into this: the duty and purpose of man in this world is to fight unceasingly against the evils that Tribulation loosed upon it. Above all, he must see that the human form is kept true to the divine pattern in order that one day it may be permited to regain the high place in which, as the image of God, it was set.

However, I did not talk much about this part of Ethics to Sophie. Not, I think, because I ever actually classified her in my mind as a Deviation; but it had to be admitted that she did not quite qualify as a true image, so it seemed more tactful to avoid that aspect. And there were plenty of other things to talk about.

Chapter Five

NOBODY AT WAKNUK seemed to trouble about me if I was out of sight. It was only when I hung about that they thought of jobs that needed doing.

The season was a good one, sunny, yet well watered so that even farmers had little to complain of other than the pressure to catch up with the work that the invasion had interrupted. Except among the sheep the average of Offenses in the spring births had been quite unusually low. The impending crops were so orthodox that the Inspector had posted only a single field, belonging to Angus Morton, for burning. Even among the vegetables there was little deviation; the *solonaceae* as usual provided most of what there was. All in all, the season would likely set up a Purity record, and condemnations were so few that even my father was pleased enough to announce guardedly in one of his addresses that Waknuk appeared to be giving the forces of Evil quite a setback this year.

With everyone so busy I was able to get away early, and during those long summer days Sophie and I roamed more widely than before, though we did our adventuring with caution, and kept it to little-used ways in order to avoid encounters. Sophie's upbringing had given her a timidity toward strangers that was almost an instinct. Almost before one was visible she vanished noiselessly. The only adult she had made friends with was Corky who looked after the steam-engine. Everyone else was dangerous.

We discovered a place up the stream where there were banks of shingle. I liked to take off my shoes, roll up my trousers, and paddle there, examining the pools and crannies. Sophie used to sit on one of the large, flat stones that shelved into the water, and watch me wistfully. Later we went there armed with two small nets that Mrs. Wender had made, and a jar for the catch. I waded about fishing for the little shrimp-like creatures that lived there while Sophie did her best to scoop them up by reaching from the bank. She did not do very well at it. After a time she gave up, and sat watching me enviously. Then, greatly daring, she pulled off a shoe, and looked at her naked foot reflectively. After a minute she pulled off the other. She rolled her cotton trousers above her knees, and stepped into the stream. She stood there for a thoughtful moment, looking down through the water at her feet on the washed pebbles. I called to her:

"Come over this way. There're lots of them here."

She waded toward me, laughing and excited.

When we had enough of it we sat on the flat rock, letting our feet dry in the sun.

"They're not really horrible, are they?" she said, regarding hers judicially.

"They're not horrible at all. They make mine look all knobbly," I told her, honestly. She was pleased about that.

A few days later we went there again. We stood the jar on the flat stone beside our shoes while we fished, and industriously scampered back to it now and then with our catch, oblivious of all else until a voice said:

"Hullo, there, David!"

I looked up, aware of Sophie standing rigid behind me.

The boy who had called stood on the bank, just above the rock where our things lay. I knew him. Alan, the son of John Ervin, the blacksmith, about two years older than I was. I kept my head.

"Oh, hullo Alan," I said, unencouragingly.

I waded to the rock and picked up Sophie's shoes.

"Catch!" I called, as I threw them to her.

One she caught, the other fell in the water, but she retrieved it.

"What are you doing?" Alan asked.

I told him we were catching the shrimp-things. As I said it I stepped casually out of the water on to the rock. I had never cared much for what I knew of Alan at the best of times, and he was by no means welcome now.

"They're no good. Fish are what you want to go after," he said, contemptuously.

He turned his attention to Sophie, who was wading to the bank, shoes in hand, some yards further up.

"Who's *she?*" he inquired.

I delayed answering while I put on my shoes. Sophie had disappeared into the bushes now.

"Who is she?" he repeated. "She's not one of the——" He broke off suddenly. I looked up and saw that he was staring down at something beside me. I turned quickly. On the flat rock was a footprint, still undried. Sophie had rested one foot there as she bent over to tip her catch into the jar. The mark was still damp enough to show the print of all six toes quite clearly. I kicked over the jar. A cascade of water and struggling shrimps poured down the rock, obliterating the footprint, but I knew, with a sickly feeling, that the harm had been done.

"Ho!" said Alan, and there was a gleam in his eye that I did not like. "Who is she?" he demanded again.

"She's a friend of mine," I told him.

"What's her name?"

I did not answer that.

"Huh, I'll soon find out, anyway," he said, with a grin.

"It's no business of yours," I told him.

He took no notice of that; he had turned and was standing looking along the bank toward the point where Sophie had disappeared into the bushes.

I ran up the stone and flung myself on him. He was bigger than I was, but it took him by surprise, and we went down together in a whirl of arms and legs. All I knew of fighting was what I had learned from a few sharp scuffles. I simply hit out, and did my furious best. My intention was to gain a few minutes for Sophie to put her shoes on and hide; if she had a little start, he would never be able to find her, as I knew from experience. Then he recovered from his first surprise and got in a couple of blows on my face which made me forget about Sophie and sent me at it, tooth and nail, on my own account.

We rolled back and forth on a patch of turf. I kept on hitting and struggling furiously, but his weight started to tell. He began to feel more sure of himself, and I more futile. However, I had gained something: I'd stopped him going after Sophie straight away. Gradually he got the upper hand, presently he was sitting astride of me, pummeling me as I squirmed. I kicked out and struggled, but there wasn't much I could do but raise my arms to protect my head. Then, suddenly, there was a yelp of anguish, and the blows ceased. He flopped down on top of me. I heaved him off, and sat up to see Sophie standing there with a large, rough stone in her hand.

"I hit him," she said proudly, and with a touch of wonderment. "Do you think he's dead?"

Alan lay white-faced and still, with the blood trickling down his cheek, but he was breathing all right, so he certainly wasn't dead.

"Oh, dear," said Sophie in sudden reaction, and dropped the stone.

We looked at Alan, and then at one another. Both of us, I think, had the impulse to do something for him, but we were afraid.

"No one must ever know. *No one,"* Mrs. Wender had said, so intensely. And now this boy did know. It frightened us.

I got up. I reached for Sophie's hand and pulled her away. "Come along," I told her urgently.

John Wender listened carefully and patiently while we told him about it.

"You're quite sure he saw? It wasn't simply that he was curious because Sophie was a stranger?" he asked at the end.

"No," I said. "He saw the footmark; that's why he wanted to catch her."

He nodded slowly.

"I see," he said, and I was surprised how calmly he said it.

He looked steadily at our faces. Sophie's eyes were big with a mixture of alarm and excitement. Mine must have been pink-rimmed, with dirty smears trailing from them. He turned his head and met his wife's gaze steadily.

"I'm afraid it's come, my dear. This is it," he said.

He got up and went round the table to her. He put his arms round her, bent down and kissed her. Tears stood in her eyes.

"Oh, Johnny, dear. Why are you so sweet to me, when all I've brought you is——?" He stopped that with another kiss.

They looked steadily into each other's eyes for a moment, then, without a word, they both turned to look at Sophie.

Mrs. Wender became her usual self again. She went briskly

to a cupboard, took out some food, and put it on the table.

"Wash first, you dirty things," she told us. "Then eat this up. Every bit of it."

While I washed I put the question I had wanted to ask often before.

"Mrs. Wender, if it's just Sophie's toes, couldn't you have cut them off when she was a little baby? I don't expect it would have hurt her much then, and nobody need have known."

"There'd have been marks, David, and when people saw them they'd know why. Now hurry up and eat that supper," she told me, and went busily off into the other room.

"We're going away," Sophie confided to me presently, through a mouthful of pie.

"Going away?" I repeated blankly.

She nodded. "Mummy said we'd have to go if anybody ever found out. We nearly did when you saw them."

"But—you mean, right away? Never come back?" I asked, in dismay.

"Yes, I think so."

I had been hungry, but I suddenly lost my appetite. I sat fiddling with the food on my plate. The sounds of bustling and bumping elsewhere in the house took on an ominous quality. I looked across the table at Sophie. In my throat there was a lump that wouldn't be swallowed.

"Where?" I asked, unhappily.

"I don't know—a long way, though," she told me.

We sat on. Sophie prattled between mouthfuls; I found it hard to swallow because of the lump. Everything was abruptly bleak to the horizon, and beyond. Nothing, I knew, was going to be quite the same ever again. The desolation of the prospect engulfed me. I had to struggle hard to keep back tears.

Mrs. Wender brought in a series of satchels and packs. I watched glumly as she dumped them close to the door, and went away again. Mr. Wender came in from outside and collected some of them. Mrs. Wender reappeared and took Sophie away into the other room. The next time Mr. Wender came for some more of the packs I followed him out.

The two horses, Spot and Sandy, were standing there patiently with some bundles already strapped onto them. I was surprised not to see the cart, and said so.

John Wender shook his head.

"A cart keeps you to the tracks; with packhorses you go where you like," he told me.

I watched him strapping more bundles on while I gathered courage.

"Mr. Wender," I said, "Please can't I come too?"

He stopped what he was doing, and turned to look at me. We faced one another for some moments, then slowly, regretfully, he shook his head. He must have seen that tears were close behind my eyes, for he put his hand on my shoulder, and let it rest there.

"Come along inside, Davie," he said, leading the way back to the house.

Mrs. Wender was back in the living room, standing in the middle of the floor, and looking round as if for things forgotten.

"He wants to come with us, Martie," said Mr. Wender.

She sat down on a stool, and held her arms out to me. I went to her, unable to speak. Looking over my head she said:

"Oh, Johnny. That awful father! I'm afraid for him."

Close to her like that I could catch her thoughts. They came faster, but easier to understand than words. I know how she felt, how she genuinely wished I could go with them, how she leaped on, without examining the reasons, to knowing that I could not and must not go with them. I had the complete answer before John Wender had put the first sentence of his reply into ordinary words.

"I know, Martie. But it's Sophie I'm afraid for—and you. If we were to be caught we'd be charged with kidnaping as well as concealment."

"If they take Sophie nothing could make things worse for me, Johnny."

"But it's not just that, dear. Once they are satisfied that we are out of the district we'll be someone else's responsibility, and they'll not bother much more about us. But if Strorm were to lose his boy there'd be hue and cry for miles around, and I doubt whether we'd have a chance of getting clear. They'd have posses out everywhere looking for us. We can't afford to increase the risk to Sophie, can we?"

Mrs. Wender was silent for some moments. I could feel her fitting the reasons into what she had known already. Presently her arm tightened round me.

"You *do* understand that, don't you, David? Your father would be so angry if you came with us that we'd have much less chance of getting Sophie away safely. *I* want you to come, but for Sophie's sake we daren't do it. Please be brave about it, David. You're her only friend, and you can help her by being brave. You will, won't you?"

The words were like a clumsy repetition. Her thoughts had been much clearer, and I had already had to accept the inevitable decesion. I could not trust myself to speak. I nodded dumbly, and let her hold me to her in a way my own mother never did.

The packing was finished a little before dusk. When everything was ready Mr. Wender took me aside.

"Davie," he said, man to man, "I know how fond you are of Sophie. You've looked after her like a hero, but now there's one more thing you can do to help her. Will you?"

"Yes," I told him. "What is it, Mr. Wender?"

"It's this. When we've gone don't go home at once. Will you stay here till tomorrow morning? That'll give us more time to get her safely away. Will you do that?"

"Yes," I said, reliably.

We shook hands on it. It made me feel stronger and more responsible—rather like I had on that first day when she twisted her ankle.

Sophie held out her hand with something concealed in it as we came back.

"This is for you, David," she said, putting it into my hand.

I looked at it. A curling lock of brown hair tied with a piece of yellow ribbon. I was still staring at it when she flung her arms around my neck and kissed me, with more determination than judgment. Her father picked her up and swung her high on top of the leading horse's load.

Mrs. Wender bent to kiss me, too.

"Good-by, David, dear." She touched my bruised cheek with a gentle forefinger. "We'll never forget," she said, and her eyes were shiny.

They set off. John Wender led the horses, with his gun slung across his back, and his left arm linked in his wife's. At the edge of the woods they paused and turned to wave. I waved back. They went on. The last I saw of them was Sophie's arm waving as the dusk beneath the trees swallowed them up.

The sun was getting high and the men were long ago out in the fields when I reached home. There was no one in the yard, but the Inspector's pony stood at the hitching post near the door, so I guessed my father would be in the house.

I hoped that I had stayed away long enough. It had been a bad night. I started it with a determinedly stout heart, but in spite of my resolutions it weakened somewhat when darkness fell. I had never before spent a night anywhere but in my own room at home. There, everything was familiar, but the Wenders' empty house seemed full of queer sounds. I managed to find some candles and light them, and when I had blown up the fire and put some more wood on, that, too, helped to make the place less lonely—but only a little less. Odd little noises kept occurring inside and outside the house.

The night stretched out before me in a prospect of terrors, yet nothing actually happened. The sounds like creeping footsteps never brought anything into view, the tapping was no predule to anything at all, nor were the occasional dragging noises. They were beyond explanation, but also, luckily, apparently beyond manifestation, too, and at length, in spite of them all I found my eyes blinking as I swayed on my stool. I summoned up courage and dared to move, very cautiously, across to the bed. I scrambled across it, and very thankfully got my back to a wall again. For a time I lay watching the candles and the uneasy shadows they cast in the corners of the room, and wondering what I should do when they were gone, when, all of a sudden, they *were* gone—and the sun was shining in.

I had found some bread for my breakfast in the Wenders' house, but I was hungry again by the time I reached home. That, however, could wait. My first intention was to get to my room unseen, with the very thin hope that my absence might not have been noticed, so that I would be able to pretend that I had merely overslept, but my luck was not running; Mary caught sight of me through the kitchen window as I was slipping across the yard. She called out:

"You come here at once. Everybody's been looking all over for you. Where've you been?" And then, without waiting for an answer, she added: "Father's on the rampage. Better go to him before he gets worse."

My father and the Inspector were in the seldom used, rather formal room at the front. I seemed to have arrived at a crucial time. The Inspector looked much as usual, but my father was thunderous.

"Come here!" he snapped, as soon as I appeared in the doorway.

I went nearer, reluctantly.

"Where've you been?" he demanded. "You've been out all night. Where?"

I did not answer.

He fired half a dozen questions at me, looking fiercer every second when I did not answer them.

"Come on now. Sullenness isn't going to help you. Who was this child—this Blasphemy—you were with yesterday?" he shouted.

I still did not reply. He glared at me. I had never seen him angrier. I felt sick with fright.

The Inspector intervened then. In a quiet, ordinary voice he said to me:

"You know, David, concealment of a Blasphemy—not reporting a human deviation—is a very, very serious thing. People go to prison for it. It is everybody's duty to report any kind of Offense to me, even if they aren't sure, so that I can decide. It's always important, and very important indeed if it is a Blasphemy. And in this case there doesn't seem to be any doubt about it, unless young Ervin was mistaken. Now he says this child you were with has six toes. Is that true?"

"No," I told him.

"He's lying," said my father.

"I see," said the Inspector calmly. "Well, then if it isn't true, it can't matter if we know who she is, can it?" he went on in a reasonable tone.

I made no reply to that. It seemed the safest way. We looked at one another.

"Surely, you see that's so? If it is *not* true——" he was going on persuasively, but my father cut him short.

"I'll deal with this. The boy's lying." To me he added: "Go to your room."

I hesitated. I knew well enough what that meant, but I knew, too, that with my father in his present mood it would happen whether I told or not. I set my jaw, and turned to go. My father followed, picking up a whip from the table as he came.

"That," said the Inspector curtly, "is my whip."

My father seemed not to hear him. The Inspector stood up.

"I said, that is *my* whip," he repeated, with a hard, ominous note in his voice.

My father checked his step. With an ill-tempered gesture he threw the whip back on the table. He glared at the Inspector, and then turned to follow me.

I don't know where my mother was, perhaps she was afraid of my father. It was Mary who came, and made little comforting noises as she dressed my back. She wept a little as she helped me into bed, and then fed me some broth with a spoon. I did my best to put up a brave show in front of her, but when she had gone my tears soaked into my pillow. By now it was not so much the bodily hurts that brought them—it was bitterness, self-contempt, and abasement. In wretchedness and misery I clutched the yellow ribbon and the brown curl tight in my hand.

"I couldn't help it, Sophie," I sobbed. "I couldn't help it."

Chapter Six

IN THE EVENING, when I grew calmer, I found that Rosalind was trying to talk to me. Some of the others were anxiously asking what was the matter, too. I told them about Sophie. It wasn't a secret any more now. I could feel that they were shocked. I tried to explain that a person with a deviation—a small deviation, at any rate—wasn't the monstrosity we had been told. It did not really make any difference—not to Sophie, at any rate.

They received that very doubtfully indeed. The things we had all been taught were against their acceptance, though they knew well enough that what I was telling them must be true to me. You can't lie when you talk with your thoughts. They wrestled with the novel idea that a Deviation might not be disgusting and evil—not very successfully. In the circumstances they could not give me much consolation, and I was not sorry when one by one they dropped out and I knew that they had fallen asleep.

I was tired out myself, but sleep was a long time coming. I lay there, picturing Sophie and her parents plodding their way southward toward the dubious safety of the Fringes, and hoping desperately that they would be far enough off now for my betrayal not to hurt them.

And then when sleep did come it was full of dreams. Faces and people moved restlessly through it; scenes, too. Once more there was the one where we all stood round in the yard while my father disposed of an Offense which was Sophie, and I woke up hearing my own voice shouting to him to stop. I was afraid to go to sleep again, but I did, and that time it was quite different. I dreamt again of the great city by the sea, with its houses and streets, and the things that flew in the sky. It was years since I had dreamt that one, but it still looked just the same, and in some quite obscure way it soothed me.

My mother looked in in the morning, but she was detached and disapproving. Mary was the one who took charge, and she decreed that there was to be no getting up that day. I was to lie on my front, and not wriggle about, so that my back would heal more quickly. I took the instruction meekly for it was certainly more comfortable to do as she said. So I lay there and considered what preparation I should have to make for running away, once I was about again and the stiffness had worn off. It would, I decided, be much better to have a horse, and I spent most of the morning concocting a plan for stealing one and riding away to the Fringes.

The Inspector looked in in the afternoon, bringing with him a bag of buttery sweets. For a moment I thought of trying to get something out of him—casually, of course—about the real nature of the Fringes. After all, as an expert on Deviation he might be expected to know more about them than anyone else. On second thought, however, I decided it might be impolitic.

He was sympathetic and kindly enough, but he was on a mission. He put his questions in a friendly way. Munching one of the sweets himself, he asked me:

"How long have you known that the Wender child—what is her name, by the way?"

I told him, there was no harm in that now.

"How long have you known that Sophie deviates?"

I didn't see that telling the truth could make things much worse.

"Quite a long time," I admitted.

"And how long would that be?"

"About six months, I think," I told him.

He raised his eyebrows, and then looked serious.

"That's bad, you know," he said. "It's what we call abetting a concealment. You must have known that was wrong, didn't you?"

I dropped my gaze. I wriggled uncomfortably under his straight look, and then stopped because it made my back twinge.

"It sort of didn't seem like the things they say in church," I tried to explain. "Besides, they were awfully little toes."

The Inspector took another sweet and pushed the bag back to me.

"'——And each foot shall have five toes,'" he quoted. "You remember that?"

"Yes," I admitted, unhappily.

"Well, every part of the definition is as important as any other; and if a child doesn't come within it, then it isn't human, and that means it doesn't have a soul. It is not in the image of God, it is an imitation, and in the imitations there is always some mistake. Only God produces perfection. Although Deviations may look like us in many ways, they cannot be really human. They are something quite different."

I thought that over.

"But Sophie *isn't* really different—not in any other way," I told him.

"You'll find it easier to understand when you are older, but you do know the definition, and you must have realized Sophie deviated. Why didn't you tell your father or me about her?"

I explained about my dream of my father treating Sophie as he did one of the farm Offenses. The Inspector looked at me thoughtfully for some seconds, then he nodded:

"I see," he said. "But Blasphemies are not treated the same way as Offenses."

"What happens to them?" I asked.

But he evaded that. He went on:

"You know, it's really my duty to include your name in my report. However, as your father has already taken action, I may be able to leave it out. All the same, it is a very serious matter. The Devil sends Deviations among us to weaken us and tempt us away from Purity. Sometimes he is clever enough to make a nearly perfect imitation, so we have always to be on the lookout for the mistake he has made, however small, and when we see one it must be reported at once. You'll remember that in future, won't you?"

I avoided his eye. The Inspector was the Inspector, and an important person; all the same I could not believe that the Devil had sent Sophie. I found it hard to see how the very small toe on each foot could make that much difference.

"Sophie's my friend," I said. "My best friend."

The Inspector kept on looking at me, then he shook his head, and sighed.

"Loyalty is a great virtue, but there is such a thing as misplaced loyalty. One day you will understand the importance of a greater loyalty. The Purity of the Race——" He broke off as the door opened. My father came in.

"They got them, all three of them," he said to the Inspector, and gave a look of disgust at me.

The Inspector got up promptly, and they went out together. I stared at the closed door. The misery of self-reproach struck me so that I shook all over. I could hear myself whimpering as the tears rolled down my cheeks. I tried to stop it, but I couldn't. My hurt back was forgotten. The anguish my father's news had caused me was far more painful than that. My chest was so tight with it that it was choking me.

Presently the door opened again. I kept my face to the wall. Steps crossed the room. A hand rested on my shoulder. The Inspector's voice said:

"It wasn't that, old man. You had nothing to do with it. A patrol picked them up, quite by chance, twenty miles away."

A couple of days later I said to Uncle Axel, "I'm going to run away."

He paused in his work, and gazed thoughtfully at his saw.

"I'd not do that," he advised. "It doesn't usually work very well. Besides," he added after a pause, "where would you run to?"

"That's what I wanted to ask you," I explained.

He shook his head. "Whatever district you're in they want to see your normalcy certificate," he told me. "Then they know who you are and where you're from."

"Not in the Fringes," I suggested.

He stared at me. "Man alive, you'd not want to go to the Fringes. Why they've got nothing there, not even enough food. Most of them are half-starving, that's why they make the raids. No, you'd spend all the time there just trying to keep alive, and lucky if you did."

"But there must be some other places," I said.

"Only if you can find a ship that'll take you, and even then . . ." He shook his head again. "In my experience," he told me, "if you run away from a thing just because you don't like it, you don't like what you find either. Now, running *to* a thing, that's a different matter, but what would you want to run to? Take it from me, it's a lot better here than it is most places. No, I'm against it, Davie. In a few years' time when you're a man and can look after yourself it may be different. I reckon it'd be better to stick it out till then, anyway; much better than have them just catch you and bring you back."

There was something in that. I was beginning to learn the meaning of the word "humiliation," and did not want any more of it at present. But from what he said the question of where to go would not be easily solved even then. It looked as if it would be advisable to learn what one could of the world outside Labrador, in preparation. I asked him what it was like.

"Godless," he told me. "Very godless indeed."

It was the sort of uninformative answer my father would have given. I was disappointed to have it from Uncle Axel, and told him so. He grinned.

"All right, Davie, boy, that's fair enough. So long as you'll not chatter, I'll tell you something about it."

"You mean it's secret?" I asked, puzzled.

"Not quite that," he said. "But when people are used to believing a thing is such-and-such a way, *and* the preachers want them to believe that that's the way it is, you get no thanks for upsetting their ideas. Sailors soon found that out in Rigo, so mostly they only talk about it now to other sailors. If the rest of the people want to think it's nearly all Badlands outside, they let them; it doesn't alter the way it really is, but it does make for peace and quiet."

"My book says it's all Badlands, or bad Fringes country," I told him.

"There are other books that don't but you'll not see them about much, not even in Rigo, let alone in the backwoods here," he said. "And, mind you it doesn't do to believe everything every sailor says, either. Often you're not sure whether any couple of them are talking about the same place or not, even when they think they are. But when you've seen some of it, you begin to understand that the world's a much queerer place than it looks from Waknuk. So you'll keep it to yourself?"

I assured him I would.

"All right. Well, it's this way . . ." he began.

To reach the rest of the world (my Uncle Axel explained) you start by sailing downriver from Rigo until you get to the sea. They say that it's no good sailing on straight ahead, to the east, that is, because either the sea goes on for ever, or else it comes to an end suddenly, and you sail over the edge. Nobody knows for sure.

If you make to the northeast they say there is a great land where the plants aren't very deviational, and animals and people don't *look* deviational, but the women are very tall and strong. They rule the country entirely, and do all the work. They keep their men in cages until they are about twenty-four years old, and then eat them. They also eat shipwrecked sailors. But as no one ever seems to have met anyone who has actually been there and escaped, it's difficult to see how all that can be known. Still there it is—no one has ever come back denying it, either.

The only way I know is south—I've been south three times. To get there you keep the coast to starboard as you leave the river. After a couple of hundred miles or so you come to the Straits of Newf. As the Straits widen out you keep the coast of Newf to port and call in at Lark for fresh water—and provisions, too, if the Newf people will let you have any. After that you bear southeast a while and then south, and pick up the mainland coast again to starboard. When you reach it you find it is Badlands—or at least very bad Fringes. There's plenty growing there, but sailing close inshore you can see that nearly all of it is deviational. There are animals, too, and most of them look as if it'd be difficult to classify them as Offenses against any known kinds.

A day or two's sail further on there's plenty of Badlands coastline, with no doubt about it. Soon you're following round a big bay, and you get to where there are no gaps, it's all Badlands.

When sailors first saw those parts they were pretty scared. They felt they were leaving all Purity behind, and sailing further and further away from God, where he'd not be able to help them. Everybody knows that if you walk on Badlands you die, and they'd none of them expected ever to see them so closely with their own eyes.

And a shocking sight it must have been at first, to see how the things which are against God's laws of nature flourish there just as if they had a right to. You can see giant, distorted heads of corn growing higher than small trees; big saprophytes growing on rocks, with their roots trailing out on the wind like bunches of hair, fathoms long; in some places there are fungus colonies that you'd take at first sight for big white boulders; you can see succulents like barrels, but as big as small houses, and with spines ten feet long. There are plants which grow on the cliff tops and send thick, green cables down a hundred feet and more into the sea; and you wonder whether it's a land plant that's got to the salt water, or a sea plant that's somehow climbed ashore. There are hundreds of kinds of queer things, and scarcely a normal one among them—it's a kind of jungle of Deviations, going on for miles and miles. There don't seem to be many animals, but occasionally you catch sight of one, though you'd never be able to name it. There are a fair number of birds, though, seabirds mostly; and once or twice people have seen big things flying in the distance, too far away to make out anything except that the motion didn't look right for birds. It's a weird, evil land, and many a man who sees it suddenly understands what might happen here if it weren't for the Purity Laws and the Inspectors.

It's bad, but it isn't the worst.

Further south still you begin to find patches where only coarse plants grow, and poorly at that, and soon you begin to come to stretches of coast, and land behind it, twenty, thirty, forty miles long, maybe, where nothing grows, nothing at all.

The whole seaboard is empty—black and harsh and empty. The land behind looks like a huge desert of charcoal. Where there are cliffs they are sharp-edged, with nothing to soften them. There are no fish in the sea there, no weed either, not even slime, and when a ship has sailed there the barnacles and the fouling on her bottom drop off and leave her hull clean. You don't see any birds. Nothing moves at all, except the waves breaking on the black beaches.

It is a frightful place. Masters order their ships well out for fear of it, and very relieved the sailors are to keep clear of it.

And yet it can't always have been like that because there was one ship whose captain was foolhardy enough to sail close inshore. Her crew were able to make out great stone ruins. They all agreed that they were far too regular to be natural, and they thought they might be the remains of one of the Old People's cities. But nobody knows any more about them. Most of the men in that ship wasted away and died, and the rest were never the same afterward. No other ship has risked going close in.

For hundreds of miles the coast goes on being Badlands with stretches of the dead, black land, so far, in fact, that the first navigators gave up and turned back saying that they thought it must go on like that to the ends of the earth.

The preachers and the church people were pleased to hear it, for it was very much what they had been teaching, and for a time it made people lose interest in exploring.

But later on curiosity revived, and better-found ships sailed south again. A ship called the *Venture*, which had long been given up for lost, came sailing home to Rigo. She was battered and under-manned, her canvas was patched, her mizzen jury-rigged, and her condition foul, but she triumphantly claimed the honor of being the first to reach the lands beyond the Black Coasts. She brought back a number of objects including gold and silver and copper ornaments, and a cargo of spices to prove it. Strict churchgoers refused to touch the spices for fear they might be tainted, but other people preferred to believe that they were the kinds of spices referred to in the Bible. Whatever they were, they are profitable enough now for ships to sail south in search of them.

The lands down there aren't civilized. Mostly they don't have any sense of sin there so they don't stop Deviations; and where they do have a sense of sin, they've got it mixed up. A lot of them aren't ashamed of Mutants; it doesn't seem to worry them when children turn out wrong, provided they're right enough to live and to learn to look after themselves.

You'll find islands where the people are all thickset, and others where they're thin; there are even said to be some islands where both the men and women would be passed as true images if it weren't that some strange deviation has turned them all completely black—though even that's easier to believe than the one about a race of Deviations that has dwindled to two feet high, grown fur and a tail, and taken to living in trees.

All the same, it's queerer there than you'd ever credit. Pretty nearly anything seems possible once you've seen it. That seems blasphemous at first, but after a bit you start asking yourself, well, what real evidence have *we* got about the true image? You find that the Bible doesn't say anything to contradict the Old People being like us, but, on the other hand it doesn't give any definition of Man, either. No, the definition comes from Nicholson's *Repentances* and he admits that he was writing some generations after Tribulation came. You find yourself wondering whether he *knew* he was in the true image, or whether he only thought he was. . . .

Uncle Axel had a lot more to say about southern parts than I can remember, and it was all very interesting in its way, but it didn't tell me what I wanted to know. At last I asked him point-blank.

"Uncle Axel, are there any cities there?"

"Cities?" he repeated. "Well, here and there you'll find a town, of a kind. As big as Kentak, maybe, but built differently."

"No," I told him. "I mean big places." I described the city in my dream, but without telling him it was a dream.

He looked at me oddly. "No, I never heard of any place like that," he told me.

"Further on, perhaps. Further than you went?" I suggested.

He shook his head. "You can't go further on. The sea gets full of weed. Masses of weed with stems like cables. A ship can't make her way through it, and it's trouble enough to get clear of it once you get in it at all."

"Oh," I said. "You're quite sure there's no city?"

"Sure," he said. "We'd have heard of it by this time if there was."

I was disappointed. It sounded as if running away to the South, even if I could find a ship to take me, would be little better than running away to the Fringes. For a time I had hoped, but now I had to go back to the idea that the city I dreamt of must be one of the Old People's cities after all.

Uncle Axel went on talking about the doubts of the true image that his voyages had given him. He labored it rather a lot, and after a while he broke off to ask me directly:

"You understand, don't you Davie, why I've been telling you all this?"

I was not sure that I did. Moreover, I was reluctant to admit the flaw in the tidy, familiar orthodoxy I had been taught. I recalled a phrase which I had heard a number of times.

"You lost your faith?" I inquired.

Uncle Axel snorted, and pulled a face.

"Preacher-words!" he said, and thought for a moment. "I'm telling you," he went on, "that a lot of people saying that a thing is so doesn't *prove* it is so. I'm telling you that nobody, *nobody* really *knows* what is the true image. They all *think* they know—just as we think we know, but, for all we can prove, the Old People themselves may not have been the true image." He turned, and looked long and steadily at me again.

"So," he said, "how am I, and how is anyone to be sure that this 'difference' that you and Rosalind have does not make you something nearer to the true image than other people are? Perhaps the Old People were the image; very well then, one of the things they say about them is that they could talk to one another over long distances. Now *we* can't do that, but you and Rosalind can. Just think that over, Davie. You two *may* be nearer to the image than we are."

I hesitated for perhaps a minute, and then took a decision.

"It isn't just Rosalind and me, Uncle Axel," I told him. "There are others, too."

He was startled. He stared at me.

"Others?" he repeated. "Who are they? How many?"

I shook my head.

"I don't know who they are—not names, I mean. Names don't have any thinking-shapes, so we've never bothered. You just know who's thinking, like you know who's talking. I only found out who Rosalind was by accident."

He went on looking at me seriously, uneasily.

"How many of you?" he repeated.

"Eight," I told him. "There were nine, but one of them stopped about a month ago. That's what I wanted to ask you,

Uncle Axel, do you think somebody found out? He just stopped suddenly. We've been wondering if anybody knows. . . . You see, if they found out about him . . ." I let him draw the inference himself.

Presently he shook his head.

"I don't think so. We should be pretty sure to have heard of it. It looks to me more as if it'd be an accident of some kind, being quite sudden like that. You'd like me to try to find out?"

"Yes, please. It's made some of us afraid."

I told him what I could, which was very little. It was a relief to know that he would try to find out what had happened. Now that a month had gone by without a similar thing happening to any of the rest of us we were less anxious than we had been, but still far from easy.

Before we parted he returned to his earlier advice to remember that no one could be certain of the true image.

Later, I understood why he gave it. I realized, too, that he did not greatly care what was the true image. Whether he was wise or not in trying to forestall both the alarm and the sense of inferiority that he saw lying in wait for us when we should become better aware of ourselves and our difference, I cannot say. At any rate, I decided, for the moment, not to run away from home. The practical difficulties were clearly greater than they had seemed.

Chapter Seven

THE ARRIVAL OF MY SISTER, Petra, came as a genuine surprise to me, and a conventional surprise to everyone else.

There had been a slight, not quite attributable, sense of expectation about the house for the previous week or two, but it remained unmentioned and unacknowledged. For me, the feeling that I was being kept unaware of something afoot was unresolved until there came a night when a baby howled. It was penetrating, unmistakable, and certainly within the house, where there had been no baby the day before. But in the morning nobody referred to the sound in the night. No one, indeed, would dream of mentioning the matter openly until the Inspector should have called to issue his certificate that it was a human baby in the true image. Should it unhappily turn out to violate the image and thus be ineligible for a certificate, no mention would ever be made of it, and the whole regrettable incident would be deemed not to have occurred.

As soon as it was light my father sent a stablehand off on a horse to summon the Inspector, and, pending his arrival, the whole household tried to dissemble its anxiety by pretending we were just starting another ordinary day.

The pretense grew thinner as time went on, for the stablehand, instead of bringing back the Inspector forthwith, as was to be expected when a man of my father's position and influence was concerned, returned with a polite message that the Inspector would certainly do his best to find time to pay a call in the course of the day.

It is very unwise for even a righteous man to quarrel with his local Inspector and call him names in public. The Inspector has too many ways of hitting back.

My father became very angry, the more so since the conventions did not allow him to admit what he was angry about.

Furthermore, he was well aware that the Inspector intended him to be angry. He spent the morning hanging around the house and yard, exploding with bad temper now and then over trivial matters, so that everyone crept about on tiptoe and worked very hard indeed, in order not to attract his attention.

My sister Mary disappeared now and then toward my mother's room, and for the rest of the time tried to hide her anxiety by loudly bossing the household girls. I felt compelled to hang about in order not to miss the announcement when it should come. My father kept on prowling.

The suspense was aggravated by everyone's knowledge that on the last two similar occasions there had been no certificate forthcoming. My father must have been well aware—and no doubt the Inspector was aware of it, too—that there was plenty of silent speculation whether my father would, as the law allowed, send my mother away if this occasion should turn out to be similarly unfortunate. Meanwhile, since it would have been both impolitic and undignified to go running after the Inspector, there was nothing to be done but bear the suspense as best we could.

It was not until mid-afternoon that the Inspector ambled up on his pony. My father pulled himself together, and went out to receive him. The effort to be even formally polite nearly strangled him. Even then, the Inspector was not brisk. He dismounted in a leisurely fashion, and strolled into the house, chatting about the weather. Father, red in the face, handed him over to Mary who took him along to Mother's room. Then followed the worst wait of all.

Mary said afterward that he hemmed and hawed for an unconscionable time while he examined the baby in minutest detail. At last, however, he emerged, with an expressionless face. In the little-used sitting-room he sat down at the table and fussed for a while about getting a good point on his quill. Finally he took a form from his pouch, and in a slow, deliberate hand wrote that he officially found the child to be a true female human being, free from any detectable form of deviation. He regarded that thoughtfully for some moments, as though not perfectly satisfied. He let his hand hesitate before he actually dated and signed it, then he sanded it carefully, and handed it to my enraged father, still with a faint air of uncertainty. He had, of course, no real doubt in his mind, or he would have called for another opinion; my father was perfectly well aware of that, too.

And so Petra's existence could at last be admitted. I was formally told that I had a new sister, and presently I was taken to see her where she lay in a crib beside my mother's bed.

She looked so pink and wrinkled to me that I did not see how the Inspector could have been quite sure about her. However, there was nothing obviously wrong with her, so she had got her certificate. Nobody could blame the Inspector for that; she did appear to be as normal as a new-born baby ever looks.

While we were taking turns to look at her somebody started to ring the stable-bell in the customary way. Everyone on the farm stopped work, and very soon we were all assembled in the kitchen for prayers of thanksgiving.

Two, or it may have been three, days after Petra was born I happened upon a piece of my family's history that I would have preferred not to know.

I was sitting quietly in the room next to my parents' bedroom where my mother still lay in bed. It was a matter of chance, and strategy, too. It was the latest place that I had found to stay hidden awhile after the midday meal until the coast was clear and I could slip away without being given an afternoon job. Normally it was very convenient, though just at present its use required caution because the wattle wall between the rooms was cracked and I had to move very cautiously on tiptoe lest my mother should hear me.

On that particular day I was just thinking that I had allowed nearly enough time for people to be busy again when a two-wheeled trap drove up. As it passed the window I had a glimpse of my Aunt Harriet holding the reins.

I had only seen her eight or nine times, for she lived fifteen miles away in the Kentak direction, but what I knew of her I liked. She was some three years younger than my mother. Superficially they were not dissimilar, and yet in Aunt Harriet each feature had been a little softened, so that the effect of them all together was different. I used to feel when I looked at her that I was seeing my mother as she might have been—as, I thought, I would have liked her to be. She was easier to talk to, too; she did not have that somewhat damping manner of listening only to correct.

I edged over carefully on stockinged feet to the window, watched her tether the horse, pick a white bundle out of the trap, and carry it into the house. She cannot have met anyone, for a few seconds later her steps passed the door, and the latch of the next room clicked.

"Why Harriet!" my mother's voice exclaimed in surprise, and not altogether in approval. "So soon! You don't mean to say you've brought a tiny baby all that way!"

"I know," said Aunt Harriet's voice, accepting the reproof in my mother's tone, "—but I had to, Emily, I had to. I heard your baby had come early, so I—— Oh, there she is! Oh, she's lovely, Emily. She's a lovely baby." There was a pause. Presently she added, "Mine's lovely, too, isn't she? Isn't she a lovely darling?"

There was a certain amount of mutual congratulation which did not interest me a lot. I didn't suppose the babies looked much different from other babies, really. My mother said:

"I *am* glad, my dear. Henry must be delighted."

"Of course he is," said Aunt Harriet, but there was something wrong about the way she said it. Even I knew that. She hurried on: "She was born a week ago. I didn't know what to do. Then when I heard your baby had come early and was a girl, too, it was like God answering a prayer." She paused, and then added with a casualness which somehow failed to be casual, "You've got the certificate for her?"

"Of course." My mother's tone was sharp, ready for offense. I knew the expression which went with the tone. When she spoke again there was a disturbing quality in her voice.

"Harriet!" she demanded sharply. "Are you going to tell me that you have *not* got a certificate?"

My aunt made no reply, but I thought I caught the sound of a suppressed sob. My mother said coldly, forcibly:

"Harriet, let me see that child—properly."

For some seconds I could hear nothing but another sob or two from my aunt. Then she said, unsteadily:

"It's such a little thing, you see. It's nothing much."

"Nothing much!" snapped my mother. "You have the effrontery to bring your monster into my house, and tell me it's *nothing much!"*

"Monster!" Aunt Harriet's voice sounded as though she had been slapped. "Oh!—Oh!—Oh!——" She broke into little moanings.

After a time my mother said:

"No wonder you didn't dare to call the Inspector."

Aunt Harriet went on crying. My mother let the sobs almost die away before she said:

"I'd like to know why you have come here, Harriet? Why did you bring it here?"

Aunt Harriet blew her nose. When she spoke it was in a dull, flat voice:

"When she came—when I saw her—I wanted to kill myself. I knew they would never approve her, although it's such a little thing. But I didn't, because I thought perhaps I could save her somehow. I love her. She's a lovely baby, except for that. She is, isn't she?"

My mother said nothing. Aunt Harriet went on:

"I didn't know how, but I hoped. I knew I could keep her for a little while before they'd take her away—just the month they give you before you *have* to notify. I decided I must have her for that long at least."

"And Henry? What does he say?"

"He—he said we ought to notify at once. But I wouldn't let him—I couldn't, Emily, I *couldn't*. Dear God, not a third time! I kept her, and prayed, and prayed, and hoped. And then when I heard your baby had come early I thought perhaps God had answered my prayers."

"Indeed, Harriet," said my mother coldly, "I doubt whether that had anything to do with it. Nor," she added pointedly, "do I see what you mean."

"I thought," Aunt Harriet went on, spiritlessly now, but forcing herself to the words, "I thought that if I could leave my baby with you, and borrow yours——"

My mother gave an incredulous gasp. Apparently words eluded her.

"It would only be for a day or two; just while I could get the certificate," Aunt Harriet went doggedly on. "You are my sister, Emily, my sister, and the only person in the world who can help me to keep my baby."

She began to cry again. There was another longish pause, then my mother's voice:

"In all my life I have never heard anything so outrageous. To come here suggesting that I should enter into an immoral, a criminal conspiracy to . . . I think you must be mad, Harriet. To think that I should lend——" She broke off at the sound of my father's heavy step in the passage.

"Joseph," she told him as he entered. "Send her away. Tell her to leave the house—and take *that* with her."

"But," said my father, in a bewildered tone, "but it's Harriet, my dear."

My mother explained the situation, fully. There wasn't a sound from Aunt Harriet. At the end he demanded incredulously:

"Is this true? Is this why you've come here?"

Slowly, wearily Aunt Harriet said, "This is the third time. They'll take my baby away again like they took the others. I can't stand that—not again. Henry will turn me out, I think. He'll find another wife, who can give him proper children. There'll be nothing—nothing in the world for me—nothing. I came here hoping for sympathy and help. Emily is the only person who can help me. I—I can see now how foolish I was to hope at all. . . ."

Nobody said anything to that.

"Very well. I understand. I'll go now," she told them, in a dead voice.

My father was not a man to leave his attitude in doubt.

"I do not understand how you dared to come here, to a Godfearing house, with such a suggestion," he said. "Worse still, you don't show an ounce of shame or remorse."

Aunt Harriet's voice was steadier as she answered:

"Why should I? I've done nothing to be ashamed of. I am *not* ashamed. I am only beaten."

"Not ashamed!" repeated my father. "Not ashamed of producing a mockery of your Maker, not ashamed of trying to tempt your own sister into criminal conspiracy!" He drew a breath and launched off in pulpit style. "The enemies of God besiege us. They seek to strike at him through us. Unendingly they work to distort the true image; through our weaker vessels they attempt to defile the race. You have sinned, woman, search your heart, and you will know that you have sinned. You wear the cross on your dress to protect you, but you have not worn it always in your heart. You have not kept constant vigilance for impurity. So there has been a Deviation, and deviation, *any* deviation from the true image is blasphemy—no less. You have produced a defilement."

"One poor little baby!"

"A baby which, if you were to have your way, would grow up to breed, and, breeding, spread pollution until all around us there would be Mutants and Abominations. Shame on you, woman. Now go! Go home in humility, not defiance. Notify your child, according to law. Then do your penance that you may be cleansed. And pray. You have much to pray for. Not only have you blasphemed by producing a false image, but in your arrogance you have set yourself against the law, and sinned in intent. I am a merciful man; I shall make no charge of that. It will be for you to clean it from your conscience, to go down on your knees and pray—pray that your sin of intention, as well as your other sins, may be forgiven you."

There were two light footsteps. The baby gave a little whimper as Aunt Harriet picked it up. She came toward the door and lifted the latch, then she paused.

"I shall pray," she said. "Yes, I shall pray." She paused, then she went on, her voice steady and harder, "I shall pray God to send charity into this hideous world, and sympathy for the weak, and love for the unhappy and unfortunate. I shall ask him if it is indeed his will that a child should suffer and its soul be damned for a little blemish of the body. And I shall pray him, too, that the hearts of the self-righteous may be broken. . . ."

Then the door closed and I heard her pass slowly along the passage.

I moved cautiously back to the window, and watched her come out and lay the white bundle gently in the trap. She stood looking down on it for a few seconds, then she unhitched the horse, climbed up onto the seat, and took the bundle onto her lap, with one arm guarding it in her cloak.

She turned, and left a picture that is fixed in my mind. The baby cradled in her arm, her cloak half-open showing the upper part of the brown, braid-edged cross on her fawn dress; eyes that seemed to see nothing as they looked toward the house from a face set hard as granite.

Then she shook the reins, and drove off.

I could not help feeling a great curiosity to know what was the "little thing" that had been wrong with the baby—wondering if, perhaps, it was just an extra toe, like Sophie's. But I never found out what it was.

When they broke the news to me next day that my Aunt Harriet's body had been found in the river, no one mentioned a baby.

Chapter Eight

MY FATHER included Aunt Harriet's name in our prayers on the evening of the day the news came, but after that she was never referred to again. It was as though she had been wiped out of every memory but mine. There, however, she remained very clearly, given form at a time when I had only heard her, as an upright figure with a face drained of hope, and a voice saying clearly: "I am *not* ashamed; I am only beaten." And, too, as I had last seen her, looking up at the house.

Nobody told me how she came to die, but somehow I knew that it had not been by accident. There was a great deal that I did not understand in what I had overheard, and yet, in spite of that, it was quite the most disturbing occurrence I had known yet. It alarmed me with a sense of insecurity far greater than I had suffered over Sophie. For several nights I dreamt of Aunt Harriet lying in the river, still clasping the white bundle to her while the water swirled her hair round her pale face, and her wide-open eyes saw nothing. And I was frightened.

This had happened simply because the baby was just a bit different in some way from other babies. It had something or lacked something so that it did not exactly accord with the Definition. There was the "little thing" that made it not quite right, not quite like other people.

A Mutant, my father had called it. A Mutant! I thought of some of the poker-work texts. I recalled the address of a visiting preacher, the detestation there had been in his voice when he thundered from the pulpit: *"Accursed is the Mutant!"*

Accursed is the Mutant. The Mutant, the enemy, not only of the human race, but of all the species God had decreed; the seed of the Devil within, trying unflaggingly, eternally to come to fruition in order that it might destroy the divine order and turn our land, the stronghold of God's will upon Earth, into a lewd chaos like the Fringes; trying to make it a place without the law, like the lands in the South that Uncle Axel had spoken of, where the plants and the animals and the almost-human beings, too, brought forth travesties; where true stock had given place to unnamable creatures, abominable growths flourished, and the spirits of evil mocked the Lord with obscene fantasies.

Just a small difference, the "little thing" was the first step.

I prayed very earnestly those nights.

"Oh, God," I said, "please, please God, let me be like other people. I don't want to be different. Won't you make it so that when I wake up in the morning I'll be just like everyone else, please, God, please!"

But in the morning, when I tested myself I'd soon pick up Rosalind or one of the others, and know that the prayer hadn't altered anything. I had to get up still just the same person who had gone to bed the night before, and I had to go into the big kitchen and eat my breakfast facing the panel which had somehow stopped being just part of the furniture and seemed to stare back at me with the words: ACCURSED IS THE MUTANT IN THE SIGHT OF GOD AND MAN!

And I went on being very frightened.

After about the fifth night that praying hadn't done any good, Uncle Axel caught me leaving the breakfast table and said I'd better come along and help him mend a plow. After we'd worked on that for a couple of hours he declared a rest, so we went out of the forge to sit in the sun, with our backs against a wall. He gave me a chunk of oatcake, and we munched for a minute or two. Then he said:

"Well now, Davie, let's have it."

"Have what?" I said, stupidly.

"Whatever it is that's been making you look as if you were sickening for something the last day or two," he told me. "What's your trouble? Has somebody found out?"

"No," I said. He looked greatly relieved.

"Well, what *is* it, then?"

So I told him about Aunt Harriet and the baby. Before I had finished I was talking through tears, it was such a relief to be able to share it with someone.

"It was her face as she drove away," I explained. "I've

never seen anyone look like that before. I keep on seeing it, in the water."

I looked up at him as I finished. His face was as grim as I'd ever seen it, with the corners of his mouth pulled down.

"So that was it," he said, nodding once or twice.

"It was all because the baby was different," I repeated. "And there was Sophie, too. . . . I didn't understand properly before. I—I'm frightened, Uncle Axel. What'll they do when they find out I'm different?"

He put his hand on my shoulder.

"No one else is ever going to know about it," he told me again. "No one but me—and I'm safe."

It did not seem as reassuring now as it had been when he said it before.

"There was that one who stopped," I reminded him, "perhaps they found out about him . . . ?"

He shook his head. "I reckon you can rest easy on that, Davie. I found out there was a boy killed just about the time you said. Walter Brent his name was, about nine years old, he was fooling around when they were felling timber, and a tree got him, poor lad."

"Where?" I asked.

"About nine or ten miles away, on a farm over by Chipping," he said.

I thought back. The Chipping direction certainly fitted, and it was just the kind of accident that would account for a sudden unexplained stop. Without any illwill to the unknown Walter I hoped and thought that was the explanation.

Uncle Axel backtracked a bit.

"There's no reason at all why anyone should find out. There's nothing to show—they can only know if you let them. Learn to watch yourself, Davie, and they'll never find out."

"What *did* they do to Sophie?" I asked once more. But again he refused to be drawn on that. He went on:

"Remember what I told you. They *think* they are the true image, but they can't know for sure. And even if the Old People were the same kind as I am and they are, what of it? Where are they, and their wonderful world now?"

" 'God sent Tribulation upon them,' " I quoted.

"Sure, sure. It's easy enough to say, but not so easy to understand, especially when you've seen a bit of the world, and what it has meant. Tribulation wasn't just tempests, hurricanes, floods, and fires like the things they had in the Bible. It was like all of them together, and something a lot worse, too. It made the Black Coasts, and the ruins that glow there at night, and the Badlands. Maybe there's a precedent for that in Sodom and Gomorrah, but what I don't understand is the queer things it did to what was left."

"Except in Labrador," I suggested.

"*Not* except in Labrador, but *less* in Labrador and Newf than any other place," he corrected me. "What can it have been—this terrible thing that must have happened? And why? I can almost understand that God, made angry, might destroy all living things, or the world itself; but I don't understand this instability; these monsters—it makes no sense."

I did not see his real difficulty. After all, God, being omnipotent, could cause anything He liked. I tried to explain this to Uncle Axel, but he shook his head.

"We've got to believe that God is sane, Davie boy. We'd be lost indeed if we didn't do that. But whatever happened out there"—he waved his hand round the horizon at large—"what happened there was *not* sane, not sane at all. It was something vast, yet something beneath the wisdom of God. So what was it? What can it have been?"

"But Tribulation——" I began.

Uncle Axel moved impatiently. "A word," he said, "a rusted mirror, reflecting nothing. It'd do the preachers good to see it for themselves. They'd not understand, but they might begin to think. They might begin to ask themselves: 'What are we doing? What are we preaching? What were the Old People really like? What was it they did to bring this frightful disaster down upon themselves and all the world?' And after a bit they might begin to say: 'Are we right? Tribulation has made the world a different place; can we ever hope to build in it the kind of world the Old People lost? Should we try to? What would be gained if we were to build it up again so exactly that it culminated in another Tribulation?' For it is clear, boy, that however wonderful the Old People were, they were not too wonderful to make mistakes, and nobody knows, or is ever likely to know, where they were wise and where they were mistaken."

Much of what he was saying went right over my head, but I thought I caught its gist. I said:

"But, Uncle, if we don't try to be like the Old People and rebuild the things that have been lost, what *can* we do?"

"Well, we might try being ourselves, and build for the world that is, instead of for one that's gone," he suggested.

"I don't think I understand," I told him. "You mean not bother about the True Line or the True Image? Not mind about Deviations?"

"Not quite that," he said, and then looked sidelong at me. "You heard some heresy from your aunt; well, here's a bit more, from your uncle. What do you think it is that makes a man a man?"

I started on the Definition. He cut me off after five words.

"It is *not*!" he said. "A wax figure could have all that, and he'd still be a wax figure, wouldn't he?"

I supposed he would.

"Well, then, what makes a man a man is something *inside* him."

"A soul?" I suggested.

"No," he said, "souls are just counters for churches to collect, all the same value, like nails. No, what makes man man is mind; it's not a thing, it's a quality, and minds aren't all the same value; they're better or worse, and the better they are, the more they mean. See where we're going?"

"No," I admitted.

"It's this way, Davie. I reckon the church people are more or less right about most deviations—only not for the reasons they say. They're right because most deviations aren't any good. Say they did allow a deviation to live like us, what'd be the good of it? Would a dozen arms and legs, or a couple of heads, or eyes like telescopes give him any more of the quality that makes him a man? They would not. Man got his physical shape—the true image, they call it—before he even knew he was man at all. Like a lot of the animals he was physically pretty nearly as good as he needed to be; but he had this new quality, mind. That was the only thing he could usefully develop. It's the only way open to him now—new qualities of mind." Uncle Axel paused reflectively. "There was a doctor on my second ship who talked that way, and the more I got to thinking it over, the more I reckoned it was the way that made sense. Now, as I see it, some way or another you and Rosalind and the others have got a new quality of mind. To pray God to take it away is wrong. It's like asking him to strike you blind, or make you deaf. I know what you're up against, Davie, but there isn't any easy way out. You have to come to terms with it. You'll have to face it and decide that, since that's the way things *are* with you, what is the best use you can make of it and still keep yourselves safe?"

That evening I told the others about Walter, we were sorry about his accident; nevertheless, it was a relief to all of them to know that it had been simply an accident. One odd thing I discovered was that he was probably some kind of distant relation; my grandmother's name had been Brent.

After that, it seemed wiser for us to find out one another's names in order to prevent such an uncertainty occurring again.

There were now eight of us in all—well, when I say that I mean that there were eight who could talk in thought-shapes. There were some others who sometimes sent traces, but so weak and so limited that they did not count. They were like someone who is not quite blind, but is scarcely able to see more than to know whether it is day or night. The occasional thought-shapes we caught from them were involuntary and too fuzzy and damped to make sense.

The other six were: Michael, who lived about three miles to the north; Sally and Katherine whose homes were on neighboring farms two miles further on, and therefore across the border of the adjoining district; Mark, almost nine miles to the northwest; and Anne and Deborah, a pair of sisters living on a big farm only a mile and a half to the west. Anne, then something over thirteen, was the eldest, Walter Brent had been the youngest by six months.

Knowing who we were was our second stage in gaining confidence. It somehow increased a comforting feeling of mutual support. Gradually I found that the texts and warnings on the walls against Mutants stood out at me less vividly. They toned down and merged once more into the general background. It was not that memories of Aunt Harriet and of Sophie were dulled; it was rather that they did not jump so frighteningly and so often into my mind.

Also, I was soon helped by having a great many new things to think about.

Our schooling, as I have said, was sketchy; mostly writing, reading from a few simple books and the Bible and *Repentances*, which were not at all simple or easy to understand, and a little elementary figuring. It was not much equipment. Certainly it was far too little to satisfy Michael's parents, so they sent him to a school over in Kentak. There, he began to learn a lot of things our old ladies had never thought of. It was natural for him to want the rest of us to know about them, too. At first he was not very clear and the distance being so much more than we were used to gave us all trouble. But, presently, after a few weeks' practice, it became much sharper and better, and he was able to hand on to the rest of us pretty nearly everything he was being taught—even some of the things he did not understand properly himself became clearer when we all thought about them, so that we were able to help him a little, too. And it pleased us to know that he was almost always at the top of his class.

It was a great satisfaction to learn and know more, it helped to ease one over a lot of puzzling matters, and I began to understand many of the things Uncle Axel talked about much better; nevertheless, it brought too, the first taste of complications from which we would never again be free. Quite quickly it became difficult always to remember how much one was supposed to know. It called for conscious restraint to remain silent in the face of simple errors, to listen patiently to silly arguments based on misconceptions, to do a job in the customary way when one knew there was a better way.

There were bad moments, of course: the careless remark that raised some eyebrows, the note of impatience toward those one should respect, the incautious suggestion. But the missteps were few, for the sense of danger now lay closer to the surface in all of us. Somehow, through caution, luck, and quick recoveries we managed to escape direct suspicion and live our two diverging lives for the next six years without the sense of peril becoming sharp.

Until, in fact, the day when we discovered that the eight of us had suddenly become nine.

Chapter Nine

IT WAS A FUNNY THING about my little sister, Petra. She seemed so normal. We never suspected, not one of us. She was a happy child, and pretty from infancy, with her close golden curls. I can still see her as a brightly dressed little thing constantly dashing hither and thither at a staggering run, clasping an atrociously crosseyed doll whom she loved with uncritical passion. A toy-like creature herself, prone as any other child to bumps, tears, chuckles, solemn moments, and a very sweet trust. I loved her. Everybody, even my father, conspired to spoil her, with an endearing lack of success. Not even a wandering thought of difference crossed my mind concerning her until her sixth year. Then, abruptly, it happened.

We were harvesting. Up in the twelve-acre there were six men mowing in echelon. I had just given up my scythe to another man, and was helping with the stooking by way of a breather when, without any warning I was struck. I had never known anything like it. One moment I was contentedly, unhurriedly binding and propping up sheaves; the next, it was as if something had hit me physically, inside my head. Very likely I actually staggered under it. Then there was pain, a demand pulling like a fishhook embedded in my mind. There was no question whether or not I should go; I was obeying in a daze. I dropped the sheaf I was holding, and pelted off across the field, past a blur of amazed faces. I kept on running, I did not know why, except that it was urgent; across half the twelve-acre, into the lane, over the fence, down the slope of the East Pasture toward the river.

Pounding across the slope on a slant, I could see the field that ran down to the far side of the river, one of Angus Morton's fields, crossed by a path that led to the footbridge, and on the path was Rosalind, running like the wind.

I kept on, down to the bank, along past the footbridge, downstream toward the deeper pools. I had no uncertainty, I kept right on to the brink of the second pool, and went into a dive without a check. I came up quite close to Petra. She was in the deep water against the steep bank, holding on to a little bush. It was bent over and down, and the roots were on the point of pulling free. A couple of strokes took me near enough to catch her under the arms.

The compulsion ebbed suddenly and faded away. I towed her to an easier landing-place. When I found bottom and could stand up I saw Rosalind's startled face peering anxiously at me over the bushes.

"Who is it?" she asked, in real words, and a shaky voice. She put her hand on her forehead. "Who was able to do that?"

I told her.

"Petra?" she repeated, staring incredulously.

I carried my little sister ashore, and laid her on the grass. She was exhausted, and only semi-conscious, but there did not seem to be anything seriously wrong with her.

Rosalind came and knelt on the grass on the other side of her. We looked down at the sopping dress and the darkened, matted curls. Then we gazed across her, at one another.

"I didn't know," I told her. "I'd no idea she was one of us."

Rosalind put her hands to her face, fingertips on her temples. She shook her head slightly and looked at me from disturbed eyes.

"She isn't," she said. "Something like us, but not one of us. None of us could *command,* like that. She's something much more than we are."

Other people came running up then; some who had followed me from the twelve-acre, some from the other side, wondering what had made Rosalind go tearing out of the house as if it were on fire. I picked Petra up to carry her home. One of the men from the field looked at me in a puzzled way:

"But how did you know?" he asked. "I didn't hear a thing."

Rosalind turned an incredulous expression of surprise toward him.

"What! With the way she was yelling! I'd've thought anybody who wasn't deaf would have heard her half-way to Kentak."

The man shook his head doubtfully, but the fact that we had both apparently heard it seemed confirmation enough to make them all uncertain.

I said nothing. I was busy trying to fend off agitated thoughts from the others, telling them to wait until either I or Rosalind was alone and could attend to them without rousing suspicions.

That night, for the first time in years, I had a once-familiar dream, only this time when the knife gleamed high in my father's right hand, the Deviation that struggled in his left was not a calf, it was not Sophie, either; it was Petra. I woke up sweating with fright.

The next day I tried to send thought-shapes to Petra. It seemed to me important for her to know as soon as possible that she must not give herself away. I tried hard, but I could make no contact with her. The rest tried, too, in turn, but there was no response. I wondered whether I should try to warn her in ordinary words, but Rosalind was against that.

"It must have been panic that brought it out," she said. "If she isn't aware of it now, she probably doesn't even know it happened, so it might easily be an unnecessary danger to tell her about it at all. She's only a little over six, remember. I don't think it is fair, or safe, to burden her until it's necessary."

There was general agreement with Rosalind's view. All of us knew that it is not easy to keep on watching each word all the time, even when you've had to practice it for years. We decided to postpone telling Petra until either some occasion made it necessary, or until she was old enough to understand more clearly what we were warning her about; in the meantime we would test occasionally to see whether we could make contact with her, otherwise the matter should rest as it stood at present.

We saw no reason then why it should not continue to stand as it did for all of us—no alternative, indeed. If we did not remain hidden, we should be finished.

In the last few years we had learned more about the people around us, and the way they felt. What had seemed five or six years ago a kind of rather disquieting game, had grown grimmer as we understood more about it. Essentially, it had not changed. Our whole consideration if we were to survive must be to keep our true selves hidden; to walk, talk and live indistinguishably from other people. We had a gift, a sense which, Michael complained bitterly, should have been a blessing, but was little better than a curse. The stupidest Norm was happier; he could feel that he belonged. We did not, and because we did not, we had no positive—we were condemned to negatives, to not revealing ourselves, to not speaking when we would, to not using what we knew, to not being found out, to a life of perpetual deception, concealment, and lying. The prospect stretching out before us chafed Michael more than it did the rest of us. His imagination took him further ahead, giving him a clearer vision of what such frustrations were going to mean, but it was no better at suggesting an alternative than ours were. As far as I was concerned I was only just beginning to perceive the vacancy in our lives. It was my appreciation of danger that had sharpened as I grew up. It had become hardened one afternoon of the summer in the year before we discovered Petra.

It was a bad season, that. We had lost three fields; so had Angus Morton. Altogether there had been twenty-five field-burnings in the district. There had been a higher deviation-rate among the spring births of the stock—not only our own stock, but everyone's, and particularly among the cattle—than had been known for twenty years. There seemed to be more wild-cats of various sizes prowling out of the woods by night than there had ever been before. Every week someone was before the court charged with attempted concealment of deviational crops, or the slaughter and consumption of undeclared Offenses among stock, and to cap it all there had been no less than three district alerts on account of raids in force from the Fringes. It was just after the stand-down following the last of these that I happened across Old Jacob grumbling to himself as he forked muck in the yard.

"What is it?" I asked him, pausing beside him.

He jabbed the fork into the muck and leaned one hand on the shaft. He had been an old man forking muck ever since I could remember. I couldn't imagine that he had ever been or would be anything else. He turned to me a lined face mostly hidden in white hair and whiskers which always made me think of Elijah.

"Beans," he said. "Now my bloody beans are wrong. First my potatoes, *then* my tomatoes, *then* my lettuce, *now* my beans. Never knew a year like it. The others I've had before, but who ever heard of beans getting tribulated?"

"Are you sure?" I said.

"Sure? 'Course I am. Think I don't know the way a bean *ought* to look, at my age?"

He glared at me out of the white fuzz.

"It's certainly a bad year," I agreed.

"Bad," he said, "it's ruination. And worse to come, I reckon." He shook his head. "Aye, worse to come," he repeated, with gloomy satisfaction.

"Why?" I inquired.

"It's a judgment," he told me. "*And* they deserve it. No morals, no principles. Look at young Ted Norbat—gets a bit of a fine for hiding a litter of ten and eating all but two before he was found out. Enough to bring his father up out of his grave. Why, if *he'd* done a thing like that—not that he ever would, mind you—but *if* he had, d'you know what he'd have got?" I shook my head. "It'd have been a public shaming on a Sunday, a week of penances, *and* a tenth of all he had," he told me, forcibly.

"But God is not mocked. Bringing Tribulation down on us, again, they are, a season like this is the start; I'm glad I'm an old man and not likely to see the fall of it. But it's coming, you mark my words.

"Government regulations made by a lot of sniveling, weak-hearted, weak-witted babblers in the East. That's what the trouble is. When my father was a young man a woman who bore a child that wasn't in the image was whipped for it. If she bore three out of the image she was uncertified, outlawed, and sold. It made them careful about their Purity and their prayers. My father reckoned there was a lot less trouble with Mutants on account of it, and when there were any, they were burnt, like other Deviations."

"Burnt!" I exclaimed.

He looked at me. "Isn't that the way to cleanse Deviations?" he demanded fiercely.

"But a Mutant isn't responsible for——" I began.

" 'Isn't responsible,' " sneered the old man. "Is a tiger-cat responsible for being a tiger-cat? But you kill it. You can't afford to have it around loose. *Repentances* says to keep pure the stock of the Lord by fire, but that's not good enough for the bloody government now.

"Give me the old days when a man was allowed to do his duty and keep the place clean. Heading right for another dose of Tribulation we are now." He went on muttering, looking like an ancient, and wrathful, prophet of doom.

I asked Uncle Axel whether there were a lot of people who really felt the way old Jacob talked. He scratched his cheek, thoughtfully.

"Quite a few of the old ones. They still feel it's a personal responsibility—like it used to be before there were Inspectors. Some of the middle-aged are that way, too, but most of them are willing enough to leave it as it is. They're not so set on the forms as their fathers were. They don't reckon it matters much what way it's done so long as the Mutants don't breed and things go along all right—but give them a run of years with instability as high as it is this year, and I'd not say for certain they'd take it quietly."

"Why should the deviation-rate suddenly get high some years?" I asked him.

He shook his head. "I don't know. Something to do with the weather, they say. Get a bad winter with gales from the southwest, and up goes the deviation-rate—not the next season, but the one after that. Something comes over from the Badlands, they say. Nobody knows what, but it looks as though they're right. The old men look on it as a warning, just a reminder of Tribulation sent to keep us on the right path, and they make the most of it. Next year's going to be a bad one, too. People will listen to them more then. They'll have a sharp eye for scapegoats." He concluded by giving me a long, thoughtful look.

I had taken the hint and passed it on to the others. Sure enough the season had been almost as tribulated as the one before, and there *was* a tendency to look for scapegoats. Public feeling toward concealments was noticeably less tolerant than it had been the previous summer, and it increased the anxiety we should in any case have felt over our discovery of Petra.

For a week after the river incident we listened with extra care for any hint of suspicion about it. We found none, however. Evidently it had been accepted that both Rosalind and I, in different directions, had happened to hear cries for help which must, in any case, have been faint at the distance. We were able to relax again, but not for long. Only about a month went by before we had a new source of misgiving.

Anne announced that she was going to marry.

Chapter Ten

THERE WAS a shade of defiance in Anne, even when she told us.

At first we did not take it very seriously. We found it difficult to believe, and we did not want to believe, that she was serious. For one thing, the man was Alan Ervin, the same Alan I had fought on the bank of the stream, and who had informed on Sophie. Anne's parents ran a good farm, not a great deal smaller than Waknuk itself; Alan was the blacksmith's son, his prospects were those of becoming the blacksmith himself in his turn. He had the physique for it, he was tall and healthy, but that was about as far as he went. Quite certainly Anne's parents would be more ambitious for her than that; so we scarcely expected anything to come of it.

We were wrong. Somehow she brought her parents round to the idea, and the engagement was formally recognized. At that point we became alarmed. Abruptly, we were forced to consider some of the implications, and, young though we were, we could see enough of them to make us anxious. It was Michael who put it to Anne, first.

"You can't, Anne. For your own sake you mustn't," he told her. "It'd be like tying yourself for life to a cripple. Do think, Anne, do really think what it is going to mean."

She came back to him angrily. "I'm not a fool. Of course I've thought. I've thought more than you have. I'm a woman—I've a right to marry and have children. There are three of you and five of us. Are you saying that two of us must never marry? Never have any lives or homes of our own? If not, then two of us have got to marry Norms. I'm in love with Alan, and I intend to marry him. You ought to be grateful. It'll help to simplify things for the rest of you."

"That doesn't follow," Michael argued. "We can't be the

only ones. There must be others like us—beyond our range, somewhere. If we wait a little . . ."

"Why should I wait? It might be for years, or for always. I've got Alan, and you want me to waste years waiting for someone who may never come, or whom I may hate if he does. You want me to give up Alan, and risk being cheated of everything. Well, I didn't ask to be the way we are; but I've as much right to get what I can out of life as anyone else.

"It's you who haven't thought, Michael—or any of you. I *know* what I intend to do; the rest of you don't know what you intend to do because you're none of you in love—except David and Rosalind—and so you've none of you faced it."

That was partially true as far as it went; but if we had not faced all the problems before they arose, we were well aware of those that were constantly with us, and of those the main one was the need of dissembling, of leading all the time a suffocating half-life with our families. One of the things we looked forward to most was relief some day from that burden, and though we'd few positive ideas how it could be achieved, we could all realize that marriage to a Norm would become intolerable in a very short while. It could not be anything but a sham of a marriage when the two were separated by something wider than a different language, which had always been hidden by the one from the other. It would be misery, perpetual lack of confidence, and insecurity; there'd be the prospect of a lifetime's guarding against slips—and we knew well enough already that occasional slips were inevitable.

Anne had seen this just as well as the rest of us, but now she pretended to ignore it. She began to defy her differences by refusing to respond to us, though whether she shut her mind off altogether, or continued to listen without taking part we could not tell. We suspected the former as being more in character, but, being unsure, we were not even able to discuss among ourselves what course, if any, we ought to take. Possibly there was no active course. I myself could think of none. Rosalind, too, was at a loss.

Rosalind had grown into a tall, slim young woman, now. She was handsome, with a face one could not help watching, she was attractive, too, in the way she moved and carried herself. Several of the younger men had felt the attraction, and gravitated toward her. She was civil to them, but no more. She would not be entangled with any of them, very likely it was for that reason that she was more shocked than any of us by what Anne proposed to do.

We used to meet, discreetly and not dangerously often. No one but the others, I think, ever suspected anything between us. We had to make love in a snatched, unhappy way when we did meet, wondering miserably whether there would ever be a time when we should not have to hide ourselves. And somehow the business of Anne made us more wretched still. Marriage to a Norm, even the kindest and best of them was unthinkable for both of us.

The only other person I could turn to for advice was Uncle Axel. He knew, as did everyone else, about the forthcoming marriage, but it was news to him that Anne was one of us, and he received it lugubriously. After he had turned it over in his mind, he shook his head.

"No. It won't do, Davie. You're right there. I've been seeing these last five or six years how it wouldn't do, but I've just been hoping that maybe it'd never come to it. I reckon you're all up against a wall, or you'd not be telling me now?"

I nodded. "She wouldn't listen to us," I told him. "Now she's gone further. She won't respond at all. She says that's over She never wanted to be different from Normals, now she wants to be as like them as she can. I never knew before that anybody could not want anybody else quite like that. She's so fierce and blind about it that she simply doesn't care what may happen later. I don't see what we can do."

"You don't think that perhaps she *can* make herself live like a Norm—cut out the other altogether? It'd be too difficult?" Uncle Axel asked.

"We've thought about that, of course," I told him. "She can refuse to respond. She's doing that now, like somebody refusing to talk. But to go on with it—it'd be like taking a vow of silence for the rest of her life. I mean, she can't just make herself forget, and *become* a Norm. We can't believe that's possible. Michael told her it'd be like pretending to have only one arm because the person one wants to marry has only one arm. It wouldn't be any good—and you couldn't keep it up, either."

Uncle Axel pondered for a bit.

"You're convinced she's crazy about this Alan, quite beyond reason, I mean?" he asked.

"She's not like herself at all. She doesn't think properly any more," I told him. "Before she stopped responding her thought-shapes were all queer with it."

Uncle Axel shook his head disapprovingly again. "Women like to think they're in love when they want to marry; they feel it's a justification which helps their self-respect," he observed. "No harm in that; most of them are going to need all the illusions they can keep up, anyway. But a woman who *is* in love is a different proposition. She lives in a world where all the old perspectives have altered. She is blinkered, single-purposed, undependable in other matters. She will sacrifice anything, including herself, to one loyalty. For her, that is quite logical; for everyone else it looks not quite sane; socially it is dangerous. And when there is also a feeling of guilt to be overcome, and maybe, expiated, it is quite certainly dangerous for someone." He broke off, and reflected in silence awhile. Then he added, "It is *too* dangerous, Davie. Remorse . . . abnegation . . . self-sacrifice . . . the desire for purification . . . all pressing upon her. The sense of burden, the need for help, for someone to share the burden. . . . Sooner or later, I'm afraid, Davie. Sooner or later . . ."

I thought so, too.

"But what can we do?" I repeated, miserably.

He turned steady, serious eyes on me.

"How much are you justified in doing? One of you is set on a course to endanger the lives of all eight. Not altogether wittingly, perhaps, but none the less seriously, for all that. Even if she does intend to be loyal to you, she is deliberately risking you all for her own ends—just a few words in her sleep would be enough. Does she have a moral right to create a constant threat hanging over seven heads just because she wants to live with this man?"

I hesitated. "Well, if you put it like that——" I began.

"I *do* put it like that. *Has* she that right?"

"We've done our best to dissuade her," I evaded, inadequately.

"Listen," said Uncle Axel. "I knew a man once who was

one of a party who were adrift in a boat after their ship had burnt. They'd not much food and very little water. One of them drank sea water and went mad. He tried to wreck the boat so that they'd all drown together. He was a menace to all of them. In the end they had to throw him overboard, with the result that the other three had just enough food and water to last until they reached land. If they hadn't done it he'd have died anyway, and the rest of them, too, most likely."

I shook my head. "No," I said decisively, "we couldn't do that."

He went on looking at me steadily.

"This isn't a nice cozy world for anyone, especially not for anyone that's different," he said. "Maybe you're not the kind to survive in it, after all."

"It isn't just that," I told him. "If it were Alan you were talking about, if it would help to throw him overboard, we'd do it, but it wouldn't help. She'd understand why, and it'd only make things worse. But it's Anne you're meaning, and we can't do it—not because she's a girl, it'd be the same with any of us; we just couldn't do it. We're all too close together. It's difficult to explain . . ." I broke off, trying to think of a way of showing him what we meant to one another. There didn't seem to be any clear way of putting it, into words. I could only tell him, not very effectively.

"It wouldn't be just murder, Uncle Axel. It'd be something worse, as well; like violating part of ourselves. We couldn't do it."

"The alternative is the sword over your heads," he said.

"I know," I agreed unhappily. "But that isn't the way. A sword inside us would be worse."

I could not even discuss that solution with the others for fear that Anne might catch our thoughts; but I knew with certainty what their verdict on it would be. I knew that Uncle Axel had proposed the only practical solution; and I knew, too, its impossibility meant recognizing that nothing could be done.

Anne now transmitted nothing whatever, we caught no trace of her, but whether she had the strength of will not to receive we were still uncertain. From Deborah, her sister, we learned that she would listen only to words, and was doing her best to pretend to herself that she was a Norm in every way, but that could not give us enough confidence for us to exchange our thoughts with freedom.

And in the following weeks Anne kept it up, so that one could almost believe that she had succeeded in renouncing her difference and becoming a Norm. Her wedding-day passed with nothing amiss, and she and Alan moved into the house which her father gave them on the edge of his own land. Here and there one encountered hints that she might have been unwise to marry beneath her, but otherwise there was little comment.

During the next few months we heard scarcely anything of her. She discouraged visits from her sister as though she was anxious to cut even that last link with us. We could only hope that she was being more successful and happier than we had feared.

One of the consequences, as far as Rosalind and I were concerned, was a more searching consideration of our own troubles. Quite when it was that we had known we were going to marry one another, neither of us was able to remember. It was one of those things that seem ordained, in such proper accord with the law of nature and our own desires, that we felt we had always known it. The prospect colored our thoughts even before we acknowledged it to ourselves. To me, it had never been thinkable that anything else should happen, for when two people have grown up thinking-together as closely as we had, and when they are drawn even closer together by the knowledge of hostility all around them they can feel the need of one another even before they know they are in love.

But when they do know they are in love they suddenly know, too, that there are ways in which they differ not at all from Norms, that some of the same obstacles must be overcome.

The feud between our families which had first come into the open over the matter of the greathorses had now been established for almost a decade. My father and half-uncle Angus, Rosalind's father, had settled down to a regular guerrilla. In their efforts to score points each kept a hawk-like watch upon the other's land for the least Deviation or Offense, and both had been known for some time now to reward the informer who would bring news of irregularities in the other's territory.

It was perfectly clear to us that neither side would be anything but dead set against a union of the families.

For both of us the situation was bound to grow more difficult. Already Rosalind's mother had attempted some matchmaking; and I had seen my mother measuring one or two girls with a calculating, though so far unsatisfied eye.

We were sure that, at present, neither side had an idea of anything between us. There was only acrid communication between the Stroms and the Mortons, and the only place they could be found beneath the same roof was church. Rosalind and I met infrequently and very discreetly.

We discussed and explored lengthily for some pacific way out of the dilemma, but even when half a year had passed since Anne's marriage we were no nearer reaching it.

As for the rest of our group, we found that in that six months the first alarm had lost its edge. That is not to say that we were easy in our minds: we had never been that since we discovered ourselves, but once the crisis over Anne had passed we got used to living with a slightly increased degree of threat.

Then, one Sunday at dusk, Alan was found dead in the field-path that led to his home, with an arrow through his neck.

We had the news first from Deborah, and we listened anxiously as she tried to make contact with her sister. She used all the concentration she could manage, but it was useless. Anne's mind remained as firmly closed against us as it had been for the last eight months. Even in distress she transmitted nothing.

"I'm going over to see her," Deborah told us. "She must have someone by her."

We waited expectantly for an hour or more. Then Deborah came through again, very perturbed.

"She won't see me. She won't let me into the house. She's let a neighbor in, but not me. She screamed at me to go away."

"She must think one of us did it," came Michael's response. "Did any of you do it?—or know anything about it?"

Our denials came in emphatically, one after another.

"We've got to stop her thinking that," Michael decided. "She mustn't go on believing it. Try to get through to her."

We all tried. There was no response whatever.

"No good," Michael admitted. "You must get a note to her somehow, Deborah," he added. "Word it carefully so that she'll understand we had nothing to do with it, but so that it won't mean anything to anyone else."

"Very well. I'll try," Deborah agreed doubtfully.

Another hour passed, before we heard from her once more.

"It's no good. I gave the note to the woman's who's there, and waited. When the woman came back she said Anne just tore it up without opening it. My mother's in there now, trying to persuade her to come home."

Michael was slow in replying to that. Then he advised.

"We'd best be prepared. All of you make ready to run for it if necessary, but don't rouse any suspicions. Deborah, keep on trying to find out what you can, and let us know at once if anything happens."

I did not know what to do for the best. Petra was already in bed, and I could not rouse her without it being noticed. Besides, I was not sure that it was necessary. She certainly could not be suspected even by Anne of having had any part in the killing of Alan. It was only potentially that she could be considered one of us at all, so I made no move beyond sketching a rough plan in my mind, and trusted that I should have enough warning to get us both clear.

The house had retired for the night before Deborah came through again.

"We're going home, mother and me," she told us. "Anne's turned everyone out, and she's alone there now. Mother wanted to stay, but Anne is beside herself and hysterical. She *made* them go. They were afraid she'd be worse if they insisted on staying. She's told Mother she knows who's responsible for Alan's death, but she wouldn't name anybody.

"You think she means us? After all, it *is* possible that Alan may have had some bitter quarrel of his own that we know nothing about," Michael suggested.

Deborah was more than dubious. "If it were only that, she'd surely have let me in. She wouldn't have screamed at me to go away," she pointed out. "I'll go over early in the morning, and see if she's changed her mind."

With that we had to be content for the moment. We could relax a little for a few hours, at least.

Deborah told us later what happened the following morning.

She had got up an hour after dawn and made her way across the fields to Anne's house. When she reached it she had hesitated a little, reluctant to face the possibility of the same sort of screaming repulse that she had suffered the previous day. However, it was useless simply to stand there looking at the house; she plucked up courage and raised the knocker. The sound of it echoed inside and she waited. There was no result.

She tried the knocker again, more decisively. Still no one answered.

Deborah became alarmed. She hammered the knocker vigorously and stood listening. Then slowly and apprehensively, she lowered her hand from the knocker, and went over to the house of the neighbor who had been with Anne the previous day.

With one of the logs from the woodpile they pushed in a window, and then climbed inside. They found Anne upstairs in her bedroom, hanging from a beam.

They took her down, between them, and laid her on the bed. They were too late by some hours to help her. The neighbor covered her with a sheet.

To Deborah it was all unreal. She was dazed. The neighbor took her by the arm to lead her out. As they were leaving she noticed a folded sheet of paper lying on the table. She picked it up.

"This'll be for you, or maybe your parents," she said, putting it into Deborah's hand.

Deborah looked at it dully, reading the inscription on the outside.

"But it's not——" she began automatically.

Then she checked herself, and pretended to look at it more closely, as it occurred to her that the woman could not read.

"Oh, I see—yes, I'll give it to them," she said, and slipped into the front of her dress the message that was addressed neither to herself, nor to her parents, but to the Inspector.

The neighbor's husband drove her home. She broke the news to her parents. Then, alone in her room, the one that Anne had shared with her before she had married, she read the letter.

It denounced all of us, including Deborah herself, and even Petra. It accused us collectively of planning Alan's murder, and one of us, unspecified, of carrying it out.

Deborah read it through twice, and then carefully burnt it.

•

The tension eased for the rest of us after a day or two. Anne's suicide was a tragedy, but no one saw any mystery about it. A young wife, pregnant with her first child, thrown off her mental balance by the shock of losing her husband in such circumstances; it was a lamentable result, but understandable.

It was Alan's death that remained unattributable to anyone, and as much of a mystery to us as to the rest. Inquiries had revealed several persons who had a grudge against him, but none with a strong-enough motive for murder, nor any likely suspect who could not convincingly account for himself at the time when Alan must have been killed.

Old William Tay acknowledged the arrow to be one of his making, but then, most of the arrows in the district were of his making. It was not a competition shaft, or identifiable in any way; just a plain everyday hunting arrow such as might be found by the dozen in any house. People gossiped, of course, and speculated. From somewhere came a rumor that Anne was less devoted than had been supposed, that for the last few weeks she had seemed to be afraid of him. To the great distress of her parents it grew into a rumor that she had let fly the arrow herself, and then committed suicide out of either remorse, or the fear of being found out. But that, too, died away when, again, no sufficiently strong motive could be discovered. In a few weeks speculation found other topics. The mystery was written off as unsolvable; it might even have been an accident which the culprit dared not acknowledge.

We had kept our ears wide open for any hint of guesswork or supposition that might lead attention toward us, but there was none at all, and as the interest declined we were able to relax.

But although we felt less anxiety than we had at any time for nearly a year, an underlying effect remained, a sense of warning, with a sharpened awareness that we were set apart, with the safety of all of us lying in the hands of each.

Chapter Eleven

THE SPRING INSPECTIONS that year were propitious. Only two fields in the whole district were on the first cleansing schedule, and neither of them belonged to my father, or to Uncle Angus. The two previous years had been so bad that people who had hesitated during the first to dispose of stock with a tendency to produce deviational offspring had killed them off in the second, with the result that the normality-rate was high on that side, too. Moreover, the encouraging trend was maintained. It put new heart into people, they became more neighborly and cheerful. By the end of May there were quite a lot of bets laid that the deviation figures were going to touch a record low. Even Old Jacob had to admit that divine displeasure was in abeyance for the time being.

For us, as for everyone else, it looked like being a serene, if industrious, summer, and possibly it would have been so, but for Petra.

It was one day early in June that, inspired apparently by a feeling for adventure, she did two things she knew to be forbidden. First, although she was alone, she rode her pony off our own land; and second, she was not content to keep to the open country, but went exploring in the woods.

The woods about Waknuk are, as I have said, considered fairly safe, but it does not do to count on that. Wildcats will seldom attack unless desperate; they prefer to run away. Nevertheless, it is unwise to go into the woods without a weapon of some kind, for it is possible for larger creatures to work their way down the necks of forest which thrust out of the Fringes, almost clear across Wild Country in some places, and then slink from one tract of woodland to another.

Petra's call came as suddenly and unexpectedly as before. Though it did not have the violent, compulsive panic which it had carried last time, it was intense; the degree of distress and anxiety was enough to be highly uncomfortable at the receiving end. Furthermore, the child had no control at all. She simply radiated an emotion which blotted out everything else with a great, amphorous splodge.

I tried to get through to the others to tell them I'd attend to it, but I couldn't make contact even with Rosalind. A blotting like that is hard to describe: something like being unable to make oneself heard against a loud noise, but also something like trying to see through a fog. To make it worse, it gave no picture or hint of the cause. It was—this attempt to explain one sense in terms of others is bound to be misleading—but one might say it was something like a wordless yell of protest. Just a reflex emotion, no thought, or control. I doubted even if she knew she was doing it at all. It was instinctive. All I could tell was that it was a distress signal, and coming from some distance away. . . .

I ran from the forge where I was working, and got the gun—the one that always hung just inside the house door, ready charged and primed for an emergency. In a couple of minutes I had one of the riding horses saddled up, and was away on it. One thing as definite about the call as its quality was its direction. Once I was out on the green lane I thumped my heels and was off at a gallop toward the West Woods.

If Petra had only let up on that overpowering distresss-pattern of hers for just a few minutes—long enough to let the rest of us get in touch with one another—the consequences would have been quite different. Indeed, there might have been no consequences at all. But she did not. She kept it up, like a screen, and there was nothing one could do but make for the source of it as quickly as possible.

Some of the going wasn't good. I took a tumble at one point, and lost more time catching the horse again. Once in the woods the ground was harder, for the track was kept clear and fairly well used to save a considerable circuit. I kept on along it until I realized I had overshot. The undergrowth was too thick to allow of a direct line, so I had to turn back and hunt for another track in the right direction. There was no trouble about the direction itself; not for a moment did Petra let up. At last I found a path, a narrow, frustratingly winding affair overhung by branches beneath which I had to crouch as the horse thrust its way along, but its general trend was right. At last the ground became clearer and I could choose my own way. A quarter of a mile farther on I pushed through more undergrowth and reached an open glade.

Petra herself I did not see at first. It was her pony that caught my attention. It was lying on the far side of the glade, with its throat torn open. Working at it, ripping flesh from its haunch with such single-minded intent that it had not heard my approach, was as deviational a creature as I had seen.

The animal was a reddish-brown, dappled with both yellow and darker brown spots. Its huge pad-like feet were covered with mops of fur, matted with blood now on the forepaws, and showing long, curved claws. Fur hung from the tail, too, in a way that made it look like a huge plume. The face was round, with eyes like yellow glass. The ears wide-set and drooping, the nose almost retrousse. Two large incisors projected downward over the lower jaw, and it was using these, as well as the claws, to tear at the pony.

I started to unsling the gun from my back. The movement caught its attention. It turned its head and crouched motionless, glaring at me, with the blood glistening on the lower half of its face. Its tail rose, and waved gently from side to side. I cocked the gun and was in the act of raising it when an arrow took the creature in the throat. It leapt, writhing into the air and landed on all fours, facing me still, with its yellow eyes glaring. My horse took fright and reared, and my gun exploded into the air, but before the creature could spring, two more arrows took it, one in the hindquarters, the other in the head. It stood stock-still for a moment, and then rolled over.

Rosalind rode into the glade from my right, her bow still in her hand. Michael appeared from the other side, a fresh arrow already on his string, and his eyes fixed on the creature, making sure about it. Even though we were so close to one another, we were close to Petra, too, and she was still swamping us.

"Where is she?" Rosalind asked, in words.

We looked round and then spotted the small figure twelve feet up a young tree. She was sitting in a fork and clinging round the trunk with both arms. Rosalind rode under the tree and told her it was safe to come down. Petra went on clinging, she seemed unable to let go or to move. I dismounted, climbed the tree and helped her down until Rosalind could reach up and take her. Rosalind seated her astride her saddle in front of her, and tried to soothe her, but Petra was looking down at her own dead pony. Her distress was, if anything, intensified.

"We must stop this," I said to Rosalind. "She'll be bringing all the others here."

Michael, assured that the creature was really dead, joined us. He looked at Petra, worriedly.

"She's no idea she's doing it. It's not intelligent; she's sort of howling with fright inside. It'd be better for her to howl outwardly. Let's start by getting her where she can't see her pony."

We moved off a little, round a screen of bushes. Michael spoke to her quietly, trying to encourage her. She did not seem to understand, and there was no weakening of her distress-pattern.

"Perhaps if we were all to try the same thought pattern on her simultaneously," I suggested. "Soothing-sympathizing-relaxing. Ready?"

We tried, for a full fifteen seconds. There was just a momentary check in Petra's distress, then it crowded us down again.

"No good," said Rosalind, and let up.

The three of us regarded her helplessly. The pattern was a little changed; the incisiveness of alarm had receded, but the bewilderment and distress were still overwhelming. She began to cry. Rosalind put an arm round her and held her close to her.

"Let her have it out. It'll relax the tension," said Michael.

While we were waiting for her to calm down, the thing that I had been afraid of happened. Deborah came riding out of the trees; a moment later a boy rode in from the other side. I'd never seen him until now, but I knew he must be Mark.

We had never met as a group before. It was one of the things that we had known would be unsafe. It was almost certain that the other two girls would be somewhere on the way, too, to complete a gathering that we had decided must never happen.

Hurriedly, we explained in words what had occurred. We urged them to get away and disperse as soon as possible so that they would not be seen together; Michael, too. Rosalind and I would stay with Petra and do our best to calm her.

The three of them appreciated the situation without argument. A moment later they left us, riding off in different directions.

We went on trying to comfort and soothe Petra, with little success.

Some ten minutes later the two girls, Sally and Katherine, came pushing their way through the bushes. They, too, were on horseback, and with their bows strung. We had hoped that one of the others might have met them and turned them back, but clearly they had approached by a different route.

They came closer, staring incredulously at Petra. We explained all over again, in words, and advised them to go away. They were in the act of turning their horses when a large man on a bay mare thrust out of the trees into the open.

He reined in, and sat looking at us.

"What's going on here?" he demanded, with suspicion in his tone.

He was a stranger to me, and I did not care for the look of him. I asked what one usually asked of strangers. Impatiently he pulled out his identity tag, with the current year's punch-mark on it. I showed my own. It was established that we were neither of us outlaws.

"What's all this?" he repeated.

The temptation was to tell him to mind his own damned business, but I thought it more tactful in the circumstances to be placatory. I explained that my sister's pony had been attacked, and that we had answered her calls for help. He wasn't willing to take that at its face value. He looked at me steadily, and then turned to regard Sally and Katherine.

"Maybe. But what brought you here in such a hurry?" he asked them.

"Naturally we came when we heard the child calling," Sally told him.

"I was right behind you, and I heard no calling," he said.

Sally and Katherine looked at one another. Sally shrugged. "We did," she told him, shortly.

It seemed about time I took a hand.

"I'd have thought everyone for miles around would have heard it," I said. "The pony was screaming too, poor little brute."

I led him round the clump of bushes and showed him the ravaged pony and the dead creature. He looked surprised, as if he'd not expected that evidence, but he wasn't altogether appeased. He demanded to see Rosalind's and Petra's tags.

"What's this all about?" I asked in my turn.

"You didn't know that the Fringes have got spies out?" he said.

"I didn't," I told him. "Anyway, do we *look* like Fringes people?"

He ignored the question. "Well, they have. There's an instruction to watch for them. There's trouble working up, and the clearer you keep of the woods, the less likely you are to meet it before we all do."

He still was not satisfied. He turned to look at the pony again, then at Sally.

"I'd say it's near half an hour since that pony did any screaming. How did you two manage to come straight to this spot?"

Sally's eyes widened a little.

"Well, this was the direction it came from, and then when we got nearer we heard the little girl screaming," she said simply.

"And very good it was of you to follow it up," I put in. "You would have saved her life by doing it if we hadn't happened to be a little nearer. It's all over now, and luckily she wasn't hurt. But she's had a nasty fright and I'd better get her home. Thank you both for wanting to help."

They took that up all right. They congratulated us on Petra's escape, hoped she would soon get over the shock, and then they rode off. The man lingered. He still seemed dissatisfied and a little puzzled. There was, however, nothing for him to take a firm hold of. Presently he gave the three of us a long, searching stare, looking as if he were about to say something more, but he changed his mind. Finally he repeated his advice to keep out of the woods, and then rode off in the wake of the other two. We watched him disappear among the trees.

"Who is he?" Rosalind asked, uneasily.

I could tell her that the name on his tag had been Jerome Skinner, but no more. He was a stranger to me, and our names had not seemed to mean much to him. I would have asked Sally but for the barrier that Petra was still putting up. It gave me a strange, muffled feeling to be cut off from the rest like that, and made me wonder at the strength of purpose which enabled Anne to withdraw herself entirely for those months.

Rosalind, still with her right arm around Petra, started homeward at a walk. I collected the dead pony's saddle and bridle, pulled the arrows out of the creature, and followed them.

They put Petra to bed when I brought her in. During the late afternoon and early evening the disturbance she was making fluctuated from time to time, but it kept up naggingly until almost nine o'clock when it diminished steeply and disappeared.

"Thank goodness for that. She's gone to sleep at last," came from one of the others.

"Who was that man Skinner?" Rosalind and I inquired, anxiously and simultaneously.

Sally answered: "He's fairly new here. My father knows him. He has a farm bordering on the woods near where you were. It was just bad luck his seeing us, and of course he wondered why we were making for the trees at a gallop."

"He seemed very suspicious. Why?" asked Rosalind. "Does he know anything about thought-shapes? I didn't think any of them did."

"He can't make them, or receive them himself—I tried him hard," Sally told her.

Michael's distinctive pattern came in, inquiring what it was all about. We explained. He commented:

"Some of them do have an idea that something of the kind may be possible, but only very roughly of the kind—a sort of emotional transfer of mental impressions. They call it telepathy—at least, those who believe in it do. Most of them are pretty doubtful whether it exists at all."

"Do they think it's deviational, those who do believe it exists, I mean?" I asked.

"It's difficult to say. I don't know that the question has ever been straightly put. But, academically, there's the point that since God is able to read men's minds, the true image ought to be able to do so, too. It might be argued that it is a power that men have temporarily lost as a punishment, part of Tribulation, but I'd not like to risk myself on that argument in front of a tribunal."

"This man had an air of smelling a rat." Rosalind told him. "Has anybody else been inquisitive?"

They all gave her a "no" to that.

"Good," she replied. "But we must be careful this doesn't happen again. David will have to explain to Petra in words and try to teach her to use some self-control. If this distress of hers does occur, you must all of you ignore it, or, anyway, not answer it. Just leave it to David and me. We have to make sure we are not drawn together into a group again. We could easily be a lot less lucky than we were today. Does everybody understand and agree?"

Their assents came in, then presently the rest of them withdrew, leaving Rosalind and me to discuss how I could best tackle Petra.

I woke early the next morning, and the first thing I was aware of was Petra's distress once more. But it was different in quality now; her alarm had quite subsided, but given way to a lament for the dead pony. Nor did it have anything like the intensity of the previous day.

I tried to make contact with her, and, though she did not understand, there was a perceptible check and a trace of puzzlement for some seconds. I got out of bed, and went along to her room. She was glad to have company; the distress-pattern faded a lot as we chatted. Before I left I promised to take her fishing that afternoon.

It is not at all easy to explain in words how one can make intelligent thought-shapes. All of us had first found out for ourselves; a very crude fumbling to begin with, but then more skillful when we had discovered one another and begun to learn by practice. With Petra it was different. Already, at six and a half, she had had a power of projection in a different class from ours, and quite overwhelming—but without realization, and therefore with no control whatever. I did my best to explain to her, but even at her present age of almost eight the necessity of putting it in words that were simple enough presented a difficulty. After an hour of trying to make it clear to her while we sat on the river bank watching our floats, I still had not got anywhere much, and she was growing too bored to try to understand what I said. Another kind of approach seemed to be required.

"Let's play a game," I suggested. "You shut your eyes. Keep them shut tight, and pretend you're looking down a deep, deep well. There's nothing but dark to see. Right?"

"Yes," she said, eyelids tightly clenched.

"Good. Now, don't think of anything at all except how dark it is and how far, far away the bottom is. Just think of that, but look at the dark. Understand that?"

"Yes," she said again.

"Now watch," I told her.

I thought a rabbit for her, and made it twitch its nose. She chuckled. Well, that was one good thing, at least; it made sure that she *could* receive. I abolished the rabbit, and thought a puppy, then some chickens, and then a horse and cart. After a minute or two she opened her eyes, and looked bewildered.

"Where are they?" she asked, looking around.

"They aren't anywhere. They were just think-things," I told her. "That's the game. Now I'll shut my eyes, too. We'll both look down the well and think of nothing but how dark it is. Then it's your turn to think a picture at the bottom of the well, so that I can see it."

I played my part conscientiously and opened my mind to its most sensitive. That was a mistake. There was a flash and a glare and a general impression that I had been struck by a thunderbolt. I staggered in a mental daze, with no idea what her picture had been. The others came in, protesting bitterly. I explained what was going on.

"Well, for heaven's sake be careful, and don't let her do it again. I damned near put an axe through my foot," came aggrievedly from Michael.

"I've scalded my hand with the kettle," from Katherine.

"Lull her. Soothe her down somehow," advised Rosalind.

"She isn't unsoothed. She's perfectly tranquil. That seems to be just the way it is with her," I told them.

"Maybe, but it's a way it can't stay," Michael answered. "She must cut it down."

"I know—I'm doing my best. Perhaps you've got some ideas on how to tackle it?" I suggested.

"Well, next time warn us *before* she tries," Rosalind told me.

I pulled myself together and turned my attention to Petra again.

"You're too rough," I said. "This time make a *little* think-picture; a really little one ever so far away, in soft pretty colors. Do it slowly and gently, as if you were making it out of cobwebs."

Petra nodded, and closed her eyes again.

"Here it comes!" I warned the others, and waited, wishing it were the kind of thing one could take cover from.

It was not much worse than a minor explosion this time. It was dazzling, but I did manage to catch the shape of it.

"A fish!" I said. "A fish with a droopy tail."

Petra chuckled delightedly.

"Undoubtedly a fish," came from Michael. "You're doing fine. All you want to do now is to cut her down to about one per cent of the power in that last one before she burns our brains out."

"Now *you* show *me*," demanded Petra, and the lesson proceeded.

The following afternoon we had another session. It was a rather violent and exhausting business, but there was progress. Petra was beginning to grasp the idea of forming thought-shapes—in a childish way, as was only to be expected—but frequently recognizable in spite of distortions. The main trouble still was to keep the power down. When she became excited one was almost stunned by the impact. The rest complained that they could get no work done while we were at it; it was like trying to ignore sudden hammer-bangs inside one's head. Towards the end of the lesson I told Petra:

"Now I'm going to tell Rosalind to give you a think-picture. Just shut your eyes, like before."

"Where's Rosalind?" she asked, looking around.

"She's not here, but that doesn't matter with think-pictures. Now, look at the dark and think of nothing."

"And you others," I added mentally for the benefit of the rest, "just lay off, will you? Keep it all clear for Rosalind and don't interrupt. Go ahead, Rosalind, strong and clear."

We sat silent and receptive.

Rosalind made a pond with reeds round it. She put in several ducks, friendly, humorous-looking ducks of several colors. They swam a kind of ballet, except for one chunky, earnestly trying duck who was always a little late and a little wrong. Petra loved it. She gurgled with enjoyment. Then, abruptly, she projected her delight; it wiped out the whole thing and dazed us all again. It was wearing for everyone, but her progress was encouraging.

In the fourth lesson she learnt the trick of clearing one's mind without closing one's eyes, which was quite a step. By the end of the week we were really getting on. Her thought-shapes were still crude and unstable, but they would improve with practice. Her reception of simple forms was good, though as yet she could catch little of our projections to one another.

"Too difficult to see all at once and too quick," she said. "But I can tell whether it's you, or Rosalind, or Michael, or Sally doing it, but going so fast it gets muddled. The other ones are much *more* muddled, though."

"What other ones—Katherine and Mark?" I asked her.

"Oh, no. I can tell them. It's the other other ones. The long-way-away ones," she said, impatiently.

I decided to take it calmly.

"I don't think I know them. Who are they?"

"I don't know," she said. "Can't you hear them? They're over there, but a long, long way." She pointed to the south-west.

I thought that over for a few moments.

"Are they there now?" I asked.

"Yes, but not much," she said.

I tried my best to detect anything, and failed.

"Suppose you try to copy for me what you're getting from them?" I suggested.

She tried. There was something there, and with a quality in it which none of us had. It was not comprehensible and it was very blurred—possibly, I thought, because Petra was trying to relay something she could not understand herself. I could make nothing of it, and called Rosalind in, but she could do no better. Petra was evidently finding it an effort, so after a few minutes we decided to let it rest for the present.

In spite of Petra's continued propensity to slip at any moment into what, in terms of sound, would be a deafening bellow we all felt a proprietorial pride in her progress. There was a sense of excitement, too—rather as if we had discovered an unknown who we knew was destined to become a great singer: only it was something more important than that. . . .

"This," Michael said, "is going to be very interesting indeed—provided she doesn't break us all up before she gets control of it."

At supper, some ten days after the loss of Petra's pony, Uncle Axel asked me to come and give him a hand with truing-up a wheel, while there was still light enough. Superficially the request was casual, but there was something in his eye which made me agree without hesitation. I followed him out, and we went over behind the rick where we should neither be seen nor overheard. He put a straw between his teeth, and looked at me seriously.

"You been careless, Davie boy?" he asked.

There are plenty of ways of being careless, but only one he'd ask me about with the manner he was using.

"I don't think so," I told him.

"One of the others, maybe?" he suggested.

Again, I did not think so.

"H'm," he grunted. "Then why, would you say, has Joe Darley been asking questions about you? Any idea?"

I had no idea why, and told him so. He shook his head.

"I don't like it, boy."

"Just me—or the others, as well?" I asked.

"You and Rosalind Morton."

"Oh," I said, uneasily. "Still, if it's only Joe Darley. . . . Could it be he's heard a rumor about us, and is out to do a bit of scandal-raising?"

"Might be," Uncle Axel agreed, but reservedly. "On the other hand Joe is a fellow that the Inspector has used before now when he wants a few inquiries made on the quiet. I don't like it."

I did not care for it, either. But he had not approached either of us directly, and I did not see where else he was going to get any incriminating information. There was, I pointed out, nothing he could pin on us that brought us within any category of the Scheduled Deviations.

Uncle Axel shook his head. "Those lists are inclusive, not exclusive," he said. "You can't schedule all the million things that *may* happen—only the more frequent ones. There have to be test cases for new ones when they crop up. It's part of the Inspector's job to keep watch and call an inquiry if the information he gets seems to warrant it."

"We've thought about what might happen," I told him. "If there should be any questions they'll not be sure what they're looking for. All we'll have to do is act bewildered, just as a Norm would be. If Joe or anybody has anything it can't be more than suspicion, no solid evidence."

He did not seem reassured.

"There's Deborah," he suggested. "She was pretty much upset by her sister's suicide. Do you think she——?"

"No," I said confidently. "Quite apart from the fact that she couldn't do it without involving herself, we should have known if she were hiding anything."

"Well then, there's young Petra," he said.

I stared at him.

"How did you know about Petra?" I asked. "I never told you."

He nodded in a satisfied way. "So she *is*. I reckoned so."

"How did you find out?" I repeated anxiously, wondering who else might have had a similar idea. "Did she tell you?"

"Oh, no, I kind of came across it." He paused, then he added: "Indirectly it came from Anne. I told you it was a bad thing to let her marry that fellow. There's a type of woman who isn't content until she's made herself some man's slave and doormat—put herself completely in his power. That's the kind she was."

"You're not—you don't mean she *told* Alan about herself?" I protested.

"She did," he nodded. "She did more than that. She told him about all of you."

I stared at him incredulously.

"You can't be sure of that, Uncle Axel!"

"I am, Davie boy. Maybe she didn't intend to. Maybe it was only herself she told him about, being the kind who can't keep secrets in bed. And maybe he had to beat the names of the rest of you out of her, but he knew, all right. He knew."

"But even if he did, how did *you* know he knew?" I asked, with rising anxiety.

He said, reminiscently:

"Awhile ago there used to be a dive down on the waterfront in Rigo. It was run by a fellow called Grouth, and very profitably, too. He had a staff of three girls and two men, and they did as he said—just as he said. If he'd liked to tell what he knew one of the men would have been strung up for mutiny on the high seas, and two of the girls for murder. I don't know what the others had done, but he had the lot of them cold. It was as neat a setup for blackmail as you could find. If the men got any tips he had them. He saw to it that the girls were nice to the sailors who used the place, and whatever they got out of the sailors he had, too. I used to see the way he treated them, and the expression on his face when he watched them, kind of gloating because he'd got them, and he knew it, and they knew it. He'd only got to frown, and they danced."

Uncle Axel paused reflectively.

"You'd never think you'd come across just that expression on a man's face again in Waknuk church, of all places, would you? It made me feel a bit queer when I did. But there it was. It was on Alan's face while he studied first Rosalind, then Deborah, then you, then young Petra. He wasn't interested in anybody else. Just the four of you."

"You could have been mistaken—just an expression. . . ." I said.

"Not *that* expression. Oh, no. I knew that expression, it jerked me right back to the dive in Rigo. Besides, if I wasn't right, how do I come to know about Petra?"

"What did you do?"

"I came home and thought a bit about Grouth, and what

a comfortable life he'd been able to lead, and about one or two other things. Then I put a new string on my bow."

"So it was you!" I exclaimed.

"It was the only thing to do, Davie. Of course, I knew Anne would reckon it was one of you that had done it. But she couldn't denounce you without giving herself away and her sister, too. There was a risk there, but I had to take it."

"There certainly was a risk, and it nearly didn't come off," I said, and told him about the letter that Anne had left for the Inspector.

He shook his head. "I hadn't reckoned she'd go as far as that, poor girl," he said. "All the same, it had to be done, and quickly. Alan wasn't a fool. He'd see to it that he was covered. Before he actually began on you he'd have had a written deposition somewhere to be opened in the event of his death, and he'd see that you knew about it, too. It'd have been a pretty nasty situation for all of you."

The more I considered it, the more I realized how nasty it could have been.

"You took a big risk for us yourself, Uncle Axel," I told him.

He shrugged.

"Very little risk for me against a great deal for you," he said.

Presently, we came back to the matter in hand.

"But these inquiries can't have anything to do with Alan. That was weeks ago," I pointed out.

"What's more, it's not the kind of information he'd share with anyone if he wanted to cash in on it," agreed Uncle Axel. "There's one thing," he went on, "they can't know much, or they'd have called an inquiry already, and they'll have to be pretty damn sure of themselves before they do call one. The Inspector isn't going to put himself in a weak spot with your father, if he can help it—nor with Angus Morton, either, for that matter. But that still doesn't get us any nearer to knowing what started it."

I was pressed back again into thinking it must have something to do with the affair of Petra's pony. Uncle Axel knew of its death, of course, but not much more. It would have involved telling him about Petra herself, and we had had a tacit understanding that the less he knew about us, the less he would have to hide in case of trouble. However, now that he did know about Petra, I described the event more fully. It did not look to us to be a likely source, but for lack of any other lead he made a note of the man's name.

"Jerome Skinner," he repeated, not very hopefully. "Very well, I'll see if I can find out anything about him."

We all conferred that night, but inconclusively. Michael put it:

"Well, if you and Rosalind are quite satisfied that there's been nothing to start suspicion in your district, then I don't see that it can be traceable to anybody but that man in the forest." He used a thought-shape rather than bothering to spell out "Jerome Skinner" in letter-forms. "If he *is* the source, then he must have put his suspicions before the Inspector in this district, who will have handed it on as a routine report to the Inspector in yours. That'll mean that several people are wondering about it already, and there'll be questions going on here about Sally and Katherine. I'll see if I can find out anything tomorrow, and let you know."

"But what's the best thing for us to do?" Rosalind put in.

"Nothing at the moment," Michael advised. "If we are right about the source, then you are in two groups: Sally and Katherine in one; you, David, and Petra in the other; and the other three of us aren't involved at all. Don't do anything unusual, or you may cause them to pounce, on suspicion. If it does come to an inquiry we ought to be able to bluff it out by acting simple as we decided. But Petra's the weak spot; she's too young to understand. If they start on her and trick her and trap her, it might end up in sterilization and the Fringes for all of us.

"That makes her the key point. It'll be your job, David, to see that she isn't taken for questioning—at any cost. If you have to kill someone to prevent it, then you must. They'd not think twice about killing us if they had the excuse. Don't forget, if they move at all, they'll be doing it to exterminate us, by the slow method, if not by the fast.

"If the worst comes to the worst, and you can't save Petra, it would be kinder to kill her than let her go to sterilization and banishment to the Fringes—a lot more merciful for a child. You understand? Do the rest of you agree?"

Their agreements came in.

When I thought of little Petra, mutilated and thrust naked into Fringes country, to perish or survive as it should chance, I agreed, too.

"Very well," Michael went on. "Just to be on the safe side, then, it might be best if the four of you and Petra were to make your arrangements to run for it at a moment's notice, if it becomes necessary."

He went on explaining in more detail.

It is difficult to see what other course we could have taken. An overt move by any of us would at once have brought trouble on the rest. Our misfortune lay in our receiving the information regarding the inquiries when we did, and not two or three days earlier.

Chapter Twelve

THE DISCUSSION, and Michael's advice, made the threat of discovery seem both more real and more imminent than it had been when I talked to Uncle Axel earlier in the evening. Michael, I knew, had been increasingly anxious during the last year or so, as if he had a feeling that time was running out, and now I caught some of that sensation, too. I even went as far as making some preparations before I went to bed that night. At least, I put a bow and a couple of dozen arrows handy, and found a sack into which I put several loaves and a cheese. And I decided that next day I would make up a pack of spare clothes and boots and other things that would be useful, and hide it in some dry, convenient place outside. Then we should need some clothing for Petra, and a bundle of blankets, and something to hold drinking water, and it would not do to forget a tinder-box. . . .

I was still listing the desirable equipment in my mind when I fell asleep.

No more than three hours or so could have passed before I was wakened by the click of my latch. There was no moon, but there was starlight enough to show a small, white night-gowned figure by the door.

"David," she said. "Rosalind—"

But she did not need to tell me. Rosalind had already broken in, urgently.

"David," she was telling me, "we must get away at once—just as soon as you can. They've taken Sally and Katherine——"

Michael crowded in on her. "Hurry up, both of you, while there's time. It was a deliberate surprise. If they do know much about us, they'll have tried to time it to send a party for you, too—before you could be warned. They were at Sally's and Katherine's almost simultaneously just over ten minutes ago. Get moving, quick."

"Meet you below the mill. Hurry," Rosalind added.

I told Petra, in words:

"Get dressed as fast as you can. Overalls. And be very quiet."

Very likely she had not understood the thought-shapes in detail, but she had caught the urgency. She nodded, and slipped back into the dark passage.

I pulled on my clothes, and rolled the blankets into a bundle. I groped about in the shadows till I found the bow and arrows and the bag of food, and made for the door.

Petra was almost dressed already. I grabbed some clothes from her cupboard and rolled them in blankets.

"Don't put on your shoes yet," I whispered. "Carry them, and come tiptoe, like a cat."

Outside in the yard I put down the bundle and the sack while we both got our shoes on. Petra started to speak, but I put my finger to my lips, and gave her the thought-shape of Sheba, the black mare. She nodded, and we tiptoed across the yard. I just had the stable-door open when I caught a distant sound, and paused to listen.

"Horses," whispered Petra.

I heard them, too—several sets of hoofs and, faintly, the tinkle of bits.

There was no time to find the saddle and bridle for Sheba. We brought her out on the halter, and mounted from the block. With all I was carrying there was no room for Petra in front of me. She got up behind, and hung on round my waist.

Quietly we slipped out of the yard by the far end and started down the path to the riverbank while the hoofbeats on the upper track drew close to the house.

"Are you away?" I asked Rosalind, and let her know what was happening with us.

"I was away ten minutes ago. I had everything ready," she told me reprovingly. "We've all been trying our damnedest to reach you. It was lucky Petra happened to wake up."

Petra caught her own thought-shape, and broke in excitedly

to know what was happening. It was like a fountain of sparks.

"Gently, darling. Much more gently," protested Rosalind. "We'll tell you all about it soon." She paused a moment to get over the blinding effect.

"Sally? Katherine?" she inquired.

They responded together.

"We're being taken to the Inspector's. We're all innocent and bewildered. Is that best?"

Michael and Rosalind agreed that it was.

"We think," Sally went on, "that we ought to shut our minds to you. It will make it easier for us to act as Normals if we really don't know what is happening. So don't try to reach us, any of you."

"Very well—but we shall be open for you," Rosalind agreed. She diverted her thoughts to me. "Come along, David. There are lights up at the farm now."

"It's all right. We're coming," I told her. "It's going to take them some time in the dark to find which way we went, anyhow."

"They'll know by the stable-warmth that you can't have got far yet," she pointed out.

I looked back. Up by the house I could see a light in a window, and a lantern swinging in someone's hand. The sound of a man's voice calling came to us faintly. We had reached the riverbank now, and it was safe to urge Sheba to a trot. We kept that up for half a mile until we came to the ford, and then for another quarter-mile until we were approaching the mill. It seemed prudent to walk her past there in case anyone was awake. Beyond the wall we heard a dog on the chain, but it did not bark. Presently I caught Rosalind's feeling of relief, coming from somewhere a little ahead.

We trotted again, and a few moments later I noticed a movement under the trees of the track. I turned the mare that way, and found Rosalind waiting for us, and not only Rosalind, but her father's pair of greathorses. The massive creatures towered above us, both saddled with large pannier baskets. Rosalind was standing in one of the baskets, her bow, strung and ready to hand, laid across it.

I rode up close beneath her while she leaned out to see what I had brought.

"Hand me the blankets," she directed, reaching down. "What's in the sack?"

I told her.

"Do you mean to say that's all you've brought?" she said disapprovingly.

"There was some hurry," I pointed out.

She arranged the blankets to pad the saddle-board between the panniers. I hoisted Petra until she could reach Rosalind's hands. With a heave from both of us she scrambled up and perched herself on the blankets.

"We'd better keep together," Rosalind directed. "I've left room for you in the other pannier. You can shoot left-handed from there." She flipped over a kind of miniature rope-ladder so that it hung down the greathorse's left shoulder.

I slid off Sheba's back, turned her head for home, and gave her a smack on the flank to start her off, then I scrambled up awkwardly to the other pannier. The moment my foot was clear of the mounting-rings Rosalind pulled them up and hitched them. She gave the reins a shake, and before I was well settled in the pannier we were off, with the second greathorse following on a lead.

We trotted awhile, and then left the track for a stream. Where that was joined by another we branched off up the lesser. We left that and picked our way across boggy ground to another stream. We held on along the bed of that for perhaps half a mile or more and then turned off onto another stretch of uneven, marshy ground which soon became firmer until presently the hoofs were clinking among stones. We slowed still more while the horses picked a winding way amid rocks. I realized that Rosalind had put in some careful planning to hide our tracks. I must have projected the thought unwittingly, for she came in, somewhat coldly:

"It's a pity *you* didn't do a little more thinking and a little less sleeping."

"I made a start," I protested. "I was going to get everything fixed up today. It didn't seem all that urgent."

"And so when I tried to consult you about it, there you were, swinishly asleep. My mother and I spent two solid hours packing up these panniers and getting the saddles slung up ready for an emergency, while all you did was go on sleeping."

"Your mother?" I asked, startled. "Does she *know?*"

"She's sort of half-known, guessed something, for some time now. I don't know how much she's guessed; she never spoke about it at all. I think she felt that as long as she didn't have to admit it in words it might be all right. When I told her this evening that I thought it very likely I'd have to go, she cried; but she wasn't really surprised. She didn't try to argue, or dissuade me. I think she'd already resolved at the back of her mind that she'd have to help me one day, when the time came, and she did."

I thought that over. I could not imagine my own mother doing such a thing for Petra's sake. And yet she had cried after my Aunt Harriet had been sent away. And Aunt Harriet had been more than ready to break the Purity Laws. So had Sophie's mother. It made one wonder how many mothers there might be who were turning a blind eye toward matters that did not actually infringe the Definition of the True Image—and perhaps to things that did infringe it, if the Inspector could be dodged. I wondered, too, whether my mother would, in secret, be glad or sorry that I had taken Petra away.

We went on by the erratic route that Rosalind had picked to hide the trail. There were more stony places and more streams until finally we urged the horses up a steep bank and into the woods. Before long, we encountered a trackway running southwest. We did not care to risk the spoor of the greathorses there, and so kept along parallel with it until the sky began to show gray. Then we turned deeper into the woods until we found a glade which offered grass for the horses. There we hobbled them and let them graze.

After we had made a meal of bread and cheese Rosalind said:

"Since you slept so well earlier on, you'd better take first watch."

She and Petra settled themselves comfortably in blankets and soon dropped off.

I sat with my strung bow across my knees, and half a dozen arrows stuck handy in the ground beside me. There was nothing to be heard but the birds, occasionally a small animal moving, and the steady munchings of the greathorses. The sun rose into the thinner branches and began to give more warmth.

Every now and then I got up and prowled silently round the fringe of the glade, with an arrow ready hooked on the string. I found nothing, but it helped to keep me awake. After a couple of hours of it Michael came through:

"Where are you now?" he inquired.

I explained, as well as I could.

"Where are you heading?" he wanted to know.

"Southwest," I told him. "We thought we'd move by night and lie-up by day."

He approved of that, but:

"The devil of it is that with this Fringes scare there'll be a lot of patrols about. I don't know that Rosalind was wise to take those greathorses—if they're seen at all, word will go round like wildfire, even a hoof mark will be enough."

"Ordinary horses have the speed of them for short bursts," I acknowledged, "but they can't touch them for stamina."

"You may need that. Frankly, David, you're going to need your wits, too. There's hell to pay over this. They must have found out much more about you than we ever guessed, though they aren't on to Mark or Deborah or me yet. But it's got them very worried indeed. They're going to send posses after you. My idea is to volunteer for one of them right away. I'm going to plant a report of your having been seen making southeast. When that peters out, we'll have Mark start up another to take them northwest.

"If anyone does see you, stop him getting away with the news, at all costs. But don't shoot. There's an order going out not to use guns except when necessary, and as signals—all gunshots to be investigated."

"That's all right. We haven't a gun," I told him.

"So much the better. You can't be tempted to use one, but they think you have."

I had deliberately decided against taking a gun, partly on account of the noise, but mostly because they are slow to reload, heavy to carry, and useless if you run out of powder. Arrows haven't the range, but they are silent, and you can get a dozen and more of them off while a man is recharging a gun.

Mark came in: "I heard that. I'll have a northwest rumor ready for when it's needed."

"Good. But don't loose it till I tell you. Rosalind's asleep now, I suppose? Tell her to get in touch with me when she wakes, will you?"

I said I would, and everybody laid off projecting for a while.

I went on keeping my watch for another couple of hours, and then woke Rosalind for her turn. Petra did not stir. I lay down beside her, and was asleep in a minute or two.

Perhaps I was sleeping lightly, or it may have been just coincidence that I woke up to catch an anguished thought from Rosalind.

"I've killed him, Michael. He's quite dead. . . ." Then she slid off into a panicky, chaotic thought-shape.

Michael came in, steady and reassuring.

"Don't be scared, Rosalind. You had to do it. This is a war, between our kind and theirs. We didn't start it—we've just as much right to exist as they have. You mustn't be frightened, Rosalind, dear; you had to do it."

"What's happened?" I asked, sitting up.

They ignored me, or were too much occupied to notice.

I looked round the glade. Petra lay, asleep still, beside me; the greathorses were cropping the grass, undisturbed. Michael came in again:

"Hide him, Rosalind. Try to find a hollow, and pile leaves over him."

A pause. Then Rosalind, her panic conquered now, but with deep distress, agreeing.

I got up, picked up my bow, and walked across the glade in the direction I knew she must be. When I reached the edge of the trees it occurred to me that I was leaving Petra unprotected, so I went no further.

Presently Rosalind appeared among the bushes. She was walking slowly, cleaning an arrow on a handful of leaves as she came.

"What happened?" I repeated.

But she seemed to have lost control over her thought-shapes again, they were muddled and distorted by her emotions. When she got nearer she used words instead:

"It was a man. He had found the trail of the horses. I saw

him following them. Michael said . . . oh, I didn't want to do it, David, but what else could I do?"

Her eyes were full of tears. I put my arms around her, and let her cry on my shoulder. There was little I could do to comfort her. Nothing, but assure her as Michael had, that what she had done had been absolutely necessary.

After a little time we walked slowly back. She sat down beside the still-sleeping Petra. It occurred to me to ask:

"What about his horse, Rosalind? Did that get away?"

She shook her head.

"I don't know. I suppose he must have had one, but he was following our tracks on foot when I saw him."

I thought it better to retrace our course and find out whether he had left a horse tethered anywhere along it. I went back half a mile but found no horse, nor was there any trace of recent hoofmarks other than those of the greathorses. When I got back Petra was awake and chattering to Rosalind.

The day wore on. Nothing more came to us from Michael or the rest. In spite of what had happened it seemed better to stay where we were than to move by daylight with the risk of being seen. So we waited.

Then, in the afternoon, something did come, suddenly.

It was not a thought-shape; it had no real form; it was sheer distress, like a cry of agony. Petra gasped, and threw herself whimpering into Rosalind's arms. The impact was so sharp it hurt. Rosalind and I stared at one another, wide-eyed. My hands shook. Yet the shock was so formless that we could not tell which of the others it came from.

Then there was a jumble of pain and shame, overridden with hopeless desolation, and, among it, characteristic glimpses of forms that we knew without doubt were Katherine's. Rosalind put her hand on mine and held it tightly. We endured, while the sharpness dimmed, and the pressure ebbed away.

Presently came Sally, brokenly, in waves of love and sympathy to Katherine, then, in anguish, to the rest of us.

"They've broken Katherine. They've broken her. . . . Oh, Katherine, dear . . . you mustn't blame her, any of you. Please, please don't blame her. They're torturing her. It might have been any of us. She's all clouded now. She can't hear us. . . . Oh, Katherine, darling . . ." Her thoughts dissolved into shapeless distress.

Then there was Michael, unsteadily at first, but hardening into as rigid a form as I had ever received:

"It *is* war. Some day I'll kill them for what they've done to Katherine."

After that there was nothing for an hour or more. We did our rather unconvincing best to soothe and reassure Petra. She understood little of what had passed between us, but she had caught the intensity and that had been enough to frighten her.

Then there was Sally again; dully, miserably forcing herself to it:

"Katherine has admitted it; confessed. I have confirmed it. They would have forced me to it, too, in the end. I——" she hesitated, wavering. "I couldn't face it. Not the hot irons; not for nothing, when she had told them. I couldn't . . . forgive me, all of you . . . forgive us both . . ." She broke off again.

Michael came in unsteadily, anxiously, too.

"Sally, dear, of course we're not blaming you—either of you. We understand. But we must know what you've told them. How much do they know?"

"About thought-shapes—and David and Rosalind. They were nearly sure about them, but they wanted it confirmed."

"Petra, too?"

"Yes. . . . Oh, oh, oh . . . !" There was an unshaped surge of remorse. "We had to—poor little Petra—but they know, really. It was the only reason that David and Rosalind would have taken her with them. No lie would cover it."

"Anyone else?"

"No. We've told them that there isn't anyone else. I think they believe it. They are still asking questions. Trying to understand more about it. They want to know how we make thought-shapes, and what the range is. I'm telling them lies. Not more than five miles, I'm saying, and pretending it's not at all easy to understand thought-shapes even that far away. . . . Katherine's barely conscious. She can't send to you. But they keep on asking us both questions, on and on. . . . If you could see what they've done to her . . . oh, Katherine, darling . . . her feet, Michael—oh, her poor, poor feet . . ."

Sally's patterns clouded in anguish, and then faded away.

Nobody else came in. I think we were all too deeply hurt and shocked. Words have to be chosen, and then interpreted; but thought-shapes you feel, inside you. . . .

The sun was low and we were beginning to pack up when Michael made contact again.

"Listen to me," he told us. "They're taking this very seriously indeed. They're badly alarmed over us. Usually if a Deviation gets clear of a district they let him go. Nobody can settle anywhere without proofs of identity or a very thorough examination by the local Inspector, so he's pretty well bound to end up in the Fringes, anyway. But what's got them so agitated about us is that nothing shows. We've been living among them for nearly twenty years and they didn't suspect it. We could pass for normal anywhere. So a proclamation has been posted describing the three of you and officially classifying you as deviants. That means that you are non-human and therefore not entitled to any of the rights or protections of human society. Anyone who assists you in any way is committing a criminal act; and anyone concealing knowledge of your whereabouts is also liable to punishment.

"In effect, it makes you outlaws. Anyone may shoot you on sight without penalty. There is a small reward if your deaths are reported and confirmed; but there is a very much larger reward for you if you are taken alive."

There was a pause while we took that in.

"I don't understand," said Rosalind. "If we were to promise to go away and stay away . . . ?"

"They're afraid of us. They want to capture you and learn more about us—that's why there's the large reward. It isn't just a question of the true image, though that's the way they're making it appear. What they've seen is that we could be a real danger to them. Imagine if there were a lot more of us than there are, able to think together and plan and coordinate without all their machinery of words and messages. We could outwit them all the time. They find that a very unpleasant thought, so we are to be stamped out before there can be any more of us. They see it as a matter of survival, and they may be right you know."

"Are they going to kill Sally and Katherine?"

That was an incautious question which slipped from Rosalind. We waited for a response from either of the two girls. There was none. We could not tell what that meant; they might simply have closed their minds again, or be sleeping from exhaustion, or perhaps dead already. . . . Michael thought not.

"There's little reason for that when they have them safely in their hands: it would very likely raise a lot of ill-feeling. To declare a new-born baby as non-human on its physical defects is one thing; but this is a lot more delicate. It isn't going to be easy for people who have known them for years to accept the non-human verdict at all. If they were to be killed, it would make a lot of people feel uneasy and uncertain about the authorities—much the same way as a retrospective law does."

"But *we* can be killed quite safely?" Rosalind commented, with some bitterness.

"You aren't already captives, and you aren't among people who know you. To strangers you are just non-humans on the run."

There was not much one could say to that. Michael asked: "Which way are you traveling tonight?"

"Still southwest," I told him. "We had thought of trying to find some place to stop in Wild Country, but now that any hunter is licensed to shoot us, we shall have to go on into the Fringes, I think."

"That'd be best. If you can find a place to hide-up there for a bit we'll see if we can't fake your deaths. I'll try to think of some way. Tomorrow I shall be with a search party that's going southeast. I'll let you know what it's doing. Meanwhile, if you run into anyone make sure that you shoot first."

On that we broke off. Rosalind finished packing up, and we arranged the gear to make the panniers more comfortable than they had been the previous night. Then we climbed up, I on the left again, Petra and Rosalind together in the right-hand basket this time. Rosalind reached back to give a thump on the huge flank, and we moved ponderously forward once more. Petra, who had been unusually subdued during the packing up, burst into tears, and radiated distress.

She did not, it emerged from her snuffles, want to go to the Fringes, her mind was sorely troubled by thoughts of Old Maggie, and Hairy Jack and his family and the other ominous nursery-threat characters said to lurk in those regions.

It would have been easier to pacify her had we not ourselves suffered from quite a residue of childhood apprehensions, or had we been able to advance some real idea of the region to set against its morbid reputation. As it was, we, like most people, knew too little of it to be convincing, and had to go on suffering her distress again. Admittedly it was less intense than it had been on former occasions, and experience did now enable us to put up more of a barrier against it; nevertheless, the effect was wearing. Fully half an hour passed before Rosalind succeeded in soothing away the obliterating hullabaloo. When she had, the others came in anxiously, Michael inquiring, with irritation:

"What was it this time?"

We explained.

Michael dropped his irritability, and turned his attention to Petra herself. He began telling her in slow clear thought-forms how the Fringes weren't really the bogey place that people pretended. Most of the men and women who lived there were just unfortunate and unhappy. They had been taken away from their homes, often when they were babies, or some of them who were older had had to run away from their homes simply because they didn't look like other people, and they had to live in the Fringes because there was nowhere else people would leave them alone. Some of them did look very queer and funny indeed, but they couldn't help that. It was a thing to be sorry, not frightened, about. If we had happened to have extra fingers or ears by mistake we should have been sent to the Fringes—although we should be just the same people inside as we were now. What people looked like didn't really matter a great deal, one could soon get used to it, and——

But at about this stage Petra interrupted him.

"Who is the other one?" she inquired.

"What other one? What do you mean?" he asked her.

"The somebody else who's making think-pictures all mixed up with yours," she told him.

There was a pause. I opened right out, but could not detect any thought-shapes at all. Then:

"I get nothing," came from Michael, and Mark and Deborah, too. "It must be——"

There was an impetuous strong sign from Petra. In words, it would have been an impatient "Shut up!" We subsided, and waited.

I glanced over at the other pannier. Rosalind had one arm around Petra, and was looking down at her attentively. Petra herself had her eyes shut, as though all her attention were on listening. Presently she relaxed a little.

"What is it?" Rosalind asked her.

Petra opened her eyes. Her reply was puzzled, and not very clearly shaped.

"Somebody asking questions. She's a long way, a very long, long way away, I think. She says she's had my afraid-thoughts before. She wants to know who I am, and where I am. Shall I tell her?"

There was a moment's caution. Then Michael inquiring with a touch of excitement whether we approved. We did.

"All right, Petra. Go ahead and tell her," he agreed.

"I shall have to be very loud. She's such a long way away." Petra warned us.

It was as well she did. If she had let it rip while our minds were wide open she'd have blistered them. I closed mine and tried to concentrate my attention on the way ahead of us. It helped, but it was by no means a thorough defense. The shapes were simple, as one would expect of Petra's age, but they still reached me with a violence and brilliance which dazzled and deafened me.

There was the equivalent of "Phew" from Michael when it let up; closely followed by the repeated equivalent of "Shut up!" from Petra. A pause, and then another briefly blinding interlude. When that subsided:

"Where is she?" inquired Michael.

"Over there," Petra told him.

"For goodness' sake——"

"She's pointing southwest," I explained.

"Did you ask her the name of the place, darling?" Rosalind inquired.

"Yes, but it didn't mean anything, except that there were two parts of it and a lot of water," Petra told her, in words and obscurely. "She doesn't understand where I am, either."

Rosalind suggested:

"Tell her to spell it out in letter-shapes."

"But I can't read letters," Petra objected, tearfully.

"Oh, dear, that's awkward," Rosalind admitted. "But at least we can send. I'll give you the letter-shapes one by one, and you can think them on to her. How about that?"

Petra agreed, doubtfully, to try.

"Good," said Rosalind, "Look out, everybody! Here we go again."

She pictured an "L." Petra relayed it with devastating force. Rosalind followed up with an "A" and so on, until the word was complete. Petra told us:

"She understands, but she doesn't know where Labrador is. She says she'll try to find out. She wants to send us her letter-shapes, but I said it's no good."

"But it *is,* darling. You get them from her, then you show them to us—only gently, so that we can read them."

Presently we got the first one. It was "Z." We were disappointed.

"What on earth's that?" everyone inquired at once.

"She's got it back to front. It must be 'S,' " Michael decided.

"It's not 'S', it's 'Z,' " Petra insisted, tearfully.

"Never mind them. Just go on," Rosalind told her.

The rest of the word built up.

"Well, the others are proper letters," Michael admitted. "Sealand—it must be——"

"*Not* 'S,' it's 'Z,' " repeated Petra, obstinately.

"But, darling, 'Z' doesn't mean anything. Now, Sealand obviously means a land in the sea."

"If that helps," I said doubtfully. "According to my uncle Axel there's a lot more sea than anyone would think possible."

At that point everything was blotted out by Petra conversing indignantly with the unknown. She finished to announce triumphantly: "It *is* 'Z.' She says it's different from 'S'; like the noise a bee makes."

"All right," Michael told her, pacifically, "but ask her if there is a lot of sea."

Petra came back shortly with:

"Yes. There are two parts of it, with lots of sea all around. From where she is you can see the sun shining on it for miles and miles and it's all blue——"

"In the middle of the night?" said Michael. "She's crazy."

"But it isn't night where she is. She showed me," Petra said. "It's a place with lots and lots of houses, different from Waknuk houses, and much, much bigger. And there are funny carts without horses running along the roads. And things in the air, with whizzing things on top of them——"

I was jolted to recognize the picture from the childhood dreams that I had almost forgotten. I broke in, repeating it more clearly than Petra had shown it—a fish-shaped thing, all white and shiny.

"Yes—like that," Petra agreed.

"There's something very queer about this, altogether," Michael put in. "David how on earth did you know——"

I cut him short.

"Let Petra get all she can now," I suggested. "We can sort it out later."

So again we did our best to put up a barrier between ourselves and the apparently one-sided exchange that Petra was conducting in an excited fortissimo.

We made slow progress through the forest. We were anxious not to leave traces on the rides and tracks, so that the going was poor. As well as keeping our bows ready for use we had to be alert enough not to have them swept out of our hands, and to crouch low beneath overhanging branches ourselves. The risk of meeting men was not great, but there was the chance encountering of some hunting beast. Luckily, when we did hear one it was invariably in a hurry to get away. Possibly the bulk of the greathorses was discouraging; if so, it was, at least, one advantage we could set against the distinctive spoor behind us.

The summer nights are not long in those parts. We kept on plodding until there were signs of dawn and then found another glade to rest in. There would have been too much risk in unsaddling the horses. The heavy pack-saddles and panniers would have had to be hoisted off by a pulley on a branch, and that would deprive us of any chance of a quick getaway. We simply had to hobble the horses, as on the previous day.

While we ate our food I talked to Petra about the things her friend had shown her. The more she told me, the more excited I became. Almost everything fitted in with the dreams I had had as a small boy. It was like a sudden inspiration to know that the place must really exist, that I had not simply been dreaming of the ways of the Old People, but that it really was in being now, somewhere in the world. However, Petra was tired, so that I did not question her as much as I would have liked to just then, but let her and Rosalind get to sleep.

Just after sunrise Michael came through in some agitation.

"They've picked up your trail, David. That man Rosalind shot—his dog found him, and they came across the greathorse tracks. Our lot is turning back to the southwest to join in the hunt. You'd better push on. Where are you now?"

All I could tell him was that we had calculated we must be within a few miles of Wild Country by this time.

"Then get moving," he told me. "The longer you delay the more time they'll have to get a party ahead to cut you off."

It sounded like good advice. I woke Rosalind, and explained. Ten minutes later we were on our way again, with Petra still more than half asleep. With speed now more important than concealment we kept on the first southward track that we found, and urged the horses to a ponderous trot.

The way wound somewhat with the lie of the land, but its general direction was right. We followed it for fully ten miles without trouble of any kind, but then, as we rounded a corner, we came face to face with a horseman trotting towards us barely fifty yards ahead.

Chapter Thirteen

THE MAN cannot have had a moment's doubt who we were, for even as he saw us he dropped his reins and snatched his bow from his shoulder. Before he had a shaft on the string we had both loosed at him.

The motion of the greathorse was unfamiliar, and we both shot wide. He did better. His arrow passed between us, skinning our horse's head. Again I missed, but Rosalind's second shot took his horse in the chest. It reared, almost unseating him, then turned and started to bolt away ahead of us. I sent another arrow after it, and took it in the buttock. It leapt sideways, catapulting the man into the bushes, and then sped off down the track as hard as it could go.

We passed the thrown man without checking. He cringed aside as the huge hoofs clumped by within a couple of feet of his head. At the next turn we looked back to see him sitting up, feeling his bruises. The least satisfactory part of the incident was that there was now a wounded riderless horse spreading an alarm ahead of us.

A couple of miles further on, the stretch of forest came to an abrupt end, and we found ourselves looking across a narrow, cultivated valley. There was about a mile and a half of open country before the trees began again on the far side. Most of the land was pasture, with sheep and cattle behind rail and post fences. One of the few arable fields was immediately to our left. The young crop there looked as if it might be oats, but it deviated to an extent which would have caused it to be burnt long ago at home.

The sight of it encouraged us, for it could only mean that we had reached almost to Wild Country where stock could not be kept pure.

The track led at a gentle slope down to a farm which was

little better than a cluster of huts and sheds. In the open space among them which served for a yard we could see four or five women and a couple of men gathered round a horse. They were examining it, and we had little doubt what horse it was. Evidently it had only just arrived, and they were still arguing about it. We decided to go on, rather than give them time to arm and come in search of us.

So absorbed were they in their inspection of the horse that we had covered half the distance from the trees before any of them noticed us. Then one glanced up, and the rest, too, turned to stare. They could never have seen a greathorse before, and the sight of two bearing down upon them at a canter with a thunderous rumble of hoofbeats struck them momentarily rigid with astonishment. It was the horse in their midst that broke up the tableau; it reared, whinnied, and made off, scattering them.

There was no need to shoot. The whole group scuttled for the shelter of various doorways, and we pounded through their yard unmolested.

The track bore off to the left, but Rosalind held the greathorse on a straight line ahead, toward the next stretch of forest. The rails flew aside like twigs, and we kept on at a lumbering canter across the fields, leaving a trail of broken fences behind us.

At the edge of the trees, I looked back. The people at the farm emerged from shelter and stood gesticulating and staring after us.

Three or four miles further on we came out into more open country, but not like any region we had seen before. It was dotted with bushes, and brakes, and thickets. Most of the grass was coarse and large-leafed: in some places it was monstrous, growing into giant tufts where the sharp-edged blades stood eight or ten feet high.

We wound our way among them, keeping generally southwest, for another couple of hours. Then we pushed into a copse of queer, but fair-sized trees. It offered a good hiding place, and inside were several open spaces where there grew a more ordinary kind of grass which looked as if it might make suitable fodder. We decided to rest awhile there and sleep.

I hobbled the horses while Rosalind unrolled the blankets,

and presently we were eating hungrily. It was pleasantly peaceful there until Petra put out one of her blinding communications so abruptly that I bit my tongue.

Rosalind screwed up her eyes, and put a hand to her head. "For heaven's sake, child!" she protested.

"Sorry. I forgot," said Petra perfunctorily.

She sat with her head a little on one side for a minute, then she told us:

"She wants to talk to one of you. She says will you all try to hear her while she thinks her loudest."

"All right," we agreed, "but you keep quiet, or you'll blind us."

I tried my very hardest, straining sensitivity to its utmost, but there was nothing—or as near nothing as the shimmer of a heat-haze.

We relaxed again.

"No good," I said, "you'll have to tell her we can't reach her, Petra. Look out, everyone."

We did our best to damp out the exchange that followed, then Petra brought down the force of her thoughts below the dazzle level, and started to relay those she was receiving. They had to be in very simple form so that she could copy them even when she did not understand them; they reached us rather like baby-talk, and with many repeats to make sure that we grasped them. It is scarcely possible to give any idea in words of the way it came across, but it was the over-all impression that mattered, and that reached us clearly enough.

The urgent emphasis was on importance—the importance not of us, but of Petra. At all costs she must be protected. Such a power of projection as she had was unheard-of without special training—she was a discovery of the utmost value. Help was already on the way, but until it could reach us we must play for time and safety—Petra's safety, it seemed, not our own—at all costs.

There was quite a lot more that was less clear, muddled up with it, but that main point was quite unmistakable.

"Did you get it?" I asked of the others, when it had finished.

They had. Michael responded: "This is very confusing. There is no doubt that Petra's power of projection is remarkable, compared with ours, anyway, but what she seemed to me to be putting across was that she was particularly surprised to find it among primitive people, did you notice that? It looked almost as if she were meaning us."

"She was," confirmed Rosalind. "Not a shadow of doubt about it."

"There must be some misunderstanding," I put in. "Probably Petra somehow gave her the impression we were Fringes people. As for——" I was suddenly blotted out for a moment by Petra's indignant denial. I did my best to disregard it, and went on: "As for help, there must be a misunderstanding there, too. She's somewhere southwest, and everybody knows that there are miles and miles of Badlands that way. Even if they do come to an end and she's on the other side of them, how can she possibly help?"

Rosalind refused to argue about that.

"Let's wait and find out," she suggested. "Just now, all I want is sleep."

I felt the same way, and since Petra had slept most of the time in the pannier, we told her to keep a sharp lookout and wake us at once if she heard or saw anything suspicious. Both Rosalind and I fell asleep almost before we laid our heads down.

I awoke with Petra shaking my shoulder, and saw that the sun was not far off setting.

"Michael," she explained.

I cleared my mind for him.

"They've picked up your trail again. A small farm on the edge of Wild Country. You galloped through it. Remember?"

I did. He went on:

"There's a party converging there now. They'll start to follow your tracks as soon as it's light. Better get moving soon. I don't know how it is in front of you, but there may be some men cutting across from the west to head you off. If there are, my bet is that they'll keep in smallish groups for the night. They can't risk a cordon of single sentries because there are known to be Fringes people scouting around. So, with luck, you should be able to sneak through."

"All right," I agreed wearily. Then a question I had meant

to ask before occurred to me. "What's happened to Sally and Katherine?"

"I don't know. No answer. The range is getting rather long now. Does anyone know?"

Deborah came in, made faint by the distance.

"Katherine was unconscious. There's been nothing understandable since then. Mark and I are afraid." She faded, in a foggy reluctance to continue.

"Go on," Michael told her.

"Well, Katherine's been unconscious so long we're wondering if she's dead."

"And Sally?"

This time there was even more reluctance.

"We think—we're afraid something queer must have happened to her mind. There've been just one or two little jumbles from her. Very weak, not sensible at all, so we're afraid. . . ." She faded away, in great unhappiness.

There was a pause before Michael started with hard, harsh shapes.

"You understand what that means, David? They *are* afraid of us. Ready to break us down in the attempt to find out more about us, once they can catch us. You mustn't let them get hold of Rosalind or Petra—far better to kill them yourself than let that happen to them. You understand?"

I looked at Rosalind lying asleep beside me, the red of the sunset glistening on her hair, and I thought of the anguish we had felt from Katherine. The possibility of her and Petra suffering that made me shudder.

"Yes," I told him, and the others. "Yes, I understand."

I felt their sympathy and encouragement for a while, then there was nothing.

Petra was looking at me, more puzzled than alarmed. She asked earnestly, in words:

"Why did he say you must kill Rosalind and me?"

I pulled myself together.

"That was only if they catch us," I told her, trying to make it sound as if it were the sensible and usual course in such circumstances. She considered the prospect judicially, then:

"Why?" she asked.

"Well," I tried, "you see we're different from them because

they can't make thought-shapes, and when people are different, ordinary people are afraid of them."

"Why should they be afraid of us? We aren't hurting them," she broke in.

"I'm not sure that I know why," I told her. "But they are. It's a feel-thing not a think-thing. And the more stupid they are, the more like everyone else they think everyone ought to be. And once they get afraid they become cruel and want to hurt people who are different."

"Why?" inquired Petra.

"They just do. And they'd hurt us very much if they could catch us."

"I don't see why," Petra persisted.

"It's the way things work. It's complicated and rather nasty," I told her. "You'll understand better when you're older. But the thing is, we don't want you and Rosalind to be hurt. You remember when you spilt the boiling water on your foot? Well, it'd be much worse than that. Being dead's a lot better—it's sort of like being so much asleep that they can't get at you to hurt you at all."

I looked down at Rosalind, at the gentle rise and fall of her breasts as she slept. There was a vagrant wisp of hair on her cheek; I brushed it away gently and kissed her without waking her.

Presently Petra began:

"David, when you kill me and Rosalind——"

I put an arm around her. "Hush, darling. It isn't going to happen, because we aren't going to let them catch us. Now, let's wake her up, but we won't tell her about this. She might be worried, so we'll just keep it to ourselves for a secret, shall we?"

"All right," Petra agreed.

She tugged gently at Rosalind's hair.

We decided to eat again, and then push on when it was a little darker so that there would be stars to steer by. Petra was unwontedly silent over the meal. At first I thought she was brooding upon our recent conversation, but I was wrong, it appeared; after a time she emerged from her contemplations to say, conversationally:

"Zealand must be a funny place. Everybody there can make

think-pictures—well, nearly everybody—and nobody wants to hurt anybody for doing it."

"Oh, you've been chatting while we were asleep, have you," remarked Rosalind. "I must say that makes it a lot more comfortable for us."

Petra ignored that. She went on:

"They aren't all of them very good at it, though; most of them are more like you and David," she told us kindly. "But *she's* much better at it than most of them, and she's got two babies and she thinks they will be good at it, only they're too little yet. But she doesn't think they'll be as good at it as me. She says I can make stronger think-pictures than anybody at all," she concluded, complacently.

"That doesn't surprise me one bit," Rosalind told her. "What you want to learn next is to make *good* think-pictures, instead of just noisy ones," she added, deflatingly.

Petra remained unabashed. "She says I'll get better still if I work at it, and then when I grow up I must have babies who can make strong think-pictures, too."

"Oh, you must, must you," said Rosalind. "Why? My impression of think-pictures up to now is that chiefly they bring trouble."

"Not in Zealand." Petra shook her head. "She says that everybody there *wants* to make them, and people who can't do it much work hard to get better at it."

We pondered that. I recalled Uncle Axel's tales about places beyond the Black Coasts where the Deviations thought that *they* were the true image, and anything else was a Mutant.

"*She* says," Petra amplified, "that people who can only talk with words have something missing. She says we ought to be sorry for them because however old they grow they'll never be able to understand one another much better. They'll have to be one-at-a-times always, never think-togethers."

"I can't say I feel very sorry for them at present," I remarked.

"Well, she says we ought to because they have to live very dull, stupid lives compared with think-picture people," Petra said, somewhat sententiously.

We let her prattle on. It was difficult to make sense of a lot of the things she said, and possibly she had not got them right, anyway, but the one thing that did stand out clearly was that these Zealanders, whoever and wherever they were, thought no small beans of themselves. It began to seem more than likely that Rosalind had been right when she had taken "primitive" to refer to ordinary Labrador people.

In clear starlight we set out again, still winding our way between clumps and thickets in a southwesterly direction. Out of respect for Michael's warning we were traveling as quietly as we could, with our eyes and ears alert for any signs of interception. For some miles there was nothing to be heard but the steady cushioned clumping of the greathorses' hoofs, slight creakings from the girths and panniers, and, occasionally, some small animal scuttling out of our way.

After three hours or more we began to perceive uncertainly a line of deeper darkness ahead, and presently the edge of more forest solidified to loom up like a black wall.

It was not possible in the shadow to tell how dense it was. The best course seemed to be to hold straight on until we came to it and then, if it turned out to be not easily penetrable, to work along the edge until we could find a suitable place to make an entrance.

We had come within a hundred yards of it when without any warning a gun went off to the rear, and shot whistled past us.

Both horses were startled, and plunged. I was all but flung out of my pannier. The rearing horses pulled away and the lead rope parted with a snap. The other horse bolted straight toward the forest, then thought better of it and swerved to the left. Ours pelted after it. There was nothing to be done but wedge oneself in the pannier and hang on as we tore along in a rain of clods and stones flung up by hoofs of the lead horse.

Somewhere behind us a gun fired again, and we speeded up still more. . . .

For a mile or more we hurtled on in a ponderous, earth-shaking gallop. Then there was a flash ahead and half-left. At the sound of the shot our horse sprang sideways in mid-stride, swerved right, and raced for the forest. We crouched still lower in the baskets as we crashed among the trees.

By luck alone we made the entry at a point where the bigger

trunks were well separated, but, for all that, it was a nightmare ride, with branches slapping and dragging at the panniers. The greathorse simply ploughed ahead, avoiding the larger trees, thrusting through the rest, smashing its way by sheer weight while branches and saplings cracked and snapped at the onslaught.

Inevitably the horse slowed down, but its panic determination to get away from the guns abated very little. I had to brace with arms and legs and whole body to avoid being battered to pieces in the pannier, scarcely daring to raise my head even for a quick look lest a branch should knock it off.

I could not tell whether there was any pursuit, but it seemed improbable. Not only was it darker under the trees, but a horse of ordinary size would most likely have disembowelled itself in any attempt to follow over the snapped-off stems standing up like stakes behind us.

The horse began to grow calmer; the pace and violence eased, as it started to pick its way instead of crashing through. Presently the trees on our left grew thinner. Rosalind, leaning out of her pannier, caught up the reins again and urged the creature that way. We came out obliquely upon a narrow open space where we could see the stars overhead again. Whether it was an artificial track, or a natural opening was impossible to tell in the poor light. We paused a moment wondering whether to risk it, then decided that the easier going would offset the disadvantages of easier pursuit, and turned southward along it. A crackling of branches to one side brought both of us facing round, with bows ready, but it was only the other greathorse. It came trotting out of the shadows with a whinny of pleasure, and fell into place behind us as though the rope still held it.

The country was more broken now. The trail wound, taking us round outcrops of rock, slanting down the sides of gullies to cross small streams. Sometimes there were fairly open stretches, at others the trees met overhead. Our progress was inevitably slow.

We must by now, we reckoned, be truly in the Fringes. Whether or not the pursuit would risk following us any farther we could not tell. When we tried to consult Michael there was no response, so we guessed he was asleep. It was perplexing to know whether the time had not come when we ought to get rid of the telltale greathorses—perhaps drive them on along the track while we made off in a different direction on foot. The decision was difficult to make without more information. It would be foolish to get rid of the creatures unless we were sure that the pursuit would risk coming right into Fringes country after us; but, if it did, it would gain on us quickly by making a great deal faster time in daylight than we were making now. Moreover, we were tired, and the prospect of starting to travel on foot was far from attractive. Once more we tried, and failed, to make contact with Michael. A moment later the choice was taken away from us.

We were at one of the stretches where the trees met above us, making a dark tunnel through which the horse chose its way slowly and carefully. Suddenly something dropped full on me, crushing me down in the pannier. I had no warning, no chance to use the bow. There was the weight jolting the breath out of me, then a shower of sparks in my head, and that was the end of it.

Chapter Fourteen

I CAME BACK SLOWLY, lingering for what seemed a long time only half-aware.

Rosalind was calling me, the real Rosalind, the one who dwelt inside, and showed herself too seldom. The other, the practical, capable one, was her own convincing creation, not herself. I had seen her begin to build it when she was a sensitive, fearful, yet determined child. She became aware by instinct, perhaps sooner than the rest of us, that she was in a hostile world, and deliberately equipped herself to face it. The armor had grown slowly, plate by plate. I had seen her find her weapons and become skilled with them, watched her construct a character so thoroughly and wear it so constantly that for spells she almost deceived herself.

I loved the girl one could see. I loved her tall slim shape, the poise of her neck, her small, pointed breasts, her long slim legs; and the way she moved, and the sureness of her hands, and her lips when she smiled. I loved the bronze-gold hair that felt like heavy silk in one's hand, her satin-skinned shoulders, her velvet cheeks and the warmth of her body, and the scent of her breath.

All these were easy to love—too easy; anyone must love them.

They needed her defenses: the crust of independence and indifference; the air of practical, decisive reliability; the unroused interest; the aloof manner. The qualities were not intended to endear, and at times they could hurt, but one who had seen the how and why of them could admire them, if only as a triumph of art over nature.

But now it was the under-Rosalind calling gently, forlornly, all armor thrown aside, the heart naked.

And again there are no words.

Words exist that can, used by a poet, achieve a dim monochrome of the body's love, but beyond that they fail clumsily.

My love flowed out to her, hers back to me. Mine stroked and soothed. Hers caressed. The distance—and the difference—between us dwindled and vanished. We could meet, mingle, and blend. Neither one of us existed any more; for a time there was a single being that was both. There was escape from the solitary cell; brief symbiosis, sharing all the world. . . .

No one else knew the hidden Rosalind. Even Michael and the rest caught only glimpses of her. They did not know at what cost the overt Rosalind had been wrought. None of them knew my dear, tender Rosalind longing for escape, gentleness, and love; grown afraid now of what she had built for her own protection, yet more afraid still, of facing life without it.

Duration is nothing. Perhaps it was only for an instant we were together again. The importance of a point is in its existence; it has no dimensions.

Then we were apart, and I was becoming aware of mundane things: a dim gray sky, considerable discomfort, and, presently, Michael, anxiously inquiring what had happened to me. With an effort I raked my wits together.

"I don't know. Something hit me," I told him, "but I think I'm all right now, except that my head aches, and I'm damned uncomfortable."

It was only as I replied that I perceived why I was so uncomfortable. I was still in the pannier, but sort of folded into it, and the pannier itself was still in motion.

Michael did not find that very informative. He applied to Rosalind.

"They jumped down on us from overhanging branches. Four or five of them. One landed right on top of David," she explained.

"They?" asked Michael.

"Fringes people," she told him.

I was relieved. It had occurred to me that we might have been outflanked by the others. I was on the point of asking what was happening now when Michael inquired, "Was it you they fired at last night?"

I admitted that we had been fired at, but there might have been other firing for all I know.

"No. Only one lot," he told us, with disappointment "I hoped they'd made a mistake and were on a false trail We've been called together. They think it's too risky to come farther into the Fringes in small groups. We're supposed to be all assembled to move off in four hours or so from now Round about a hundred they reckon. They've decided that if we do meet any Fringes people and give them a good hiding it'll save trouble later on, anyway. You'd better get rid of those greathorses now, you'll never cover your trail while you have them."

"A bit late for that advice," Rosalind told him. "I'm in a pannier on the first horse with my thumbs tied together, and David's all tied up in a pannier on the second."

I tried to move again, and realized for the first time what was wrong, and why I couldn't.

"Where's Petra?" asked Michael anxiously.

"Oh, she's all right. She's in the other pannier of this horse, fraternizing with the man in charge."

"What happened, exactly?" Michael demanded.

"Well, first they dropped on us and then a lot more came out of the trees and steadied up the horses. They made us get down and lifted David down. Then when they'd talked and argued for a bit, they decided to get rid of us. So they loaded us into the panniers again, like this, and put a man on each horse and sent us on, the same way we'd been going."

"Further into the Fringes, that is?"

"Yes."

"Well, at least that's the best direction," Michael commented, "What's the attitude? Threatening?"

"Oh, no. They're just being careful we don't run off. They seemed to have some idea who we were, but weren't quite sure what to do with us. They argued a bit over that, but they were much more interested in the greathorses really, I think. The man on this horse seems to be quite harmless. He's talking to Petra with an odd sort of earnestness. I'm not sure he isn't a little simple."

"Can you find out what they're intending to do with you?"

"I did ask, but I don't think he knows. He's just been told to take us somewhere."

"Well——" Michael seemed at a loss for once. "Well, I

suppose all we can do is wait and see, but it'll do no harm to let him know we'll be coming after you."

He left it at that for the moment.

I struggled and wriggled round. My wrists were tied together behind my back, but my feet were free, and with some difficulty I managed to get on to them at last and stand up in the swaying basket. The man in the other pannier looked around at me quite amiably.

"Whoa, there!" he said to the greathorse, and reined in.

I was able to see our surroundings now. It was broken country, no longer thick forest, though well wooded, and even a first look at it assured me that my father had been right about normality being mocked in these parts. I could scarcely identify a single tree with certainty. There were familiar trunks supporting the wrong shape of tree: familiar types of branches growing out of the wrong kind of bark, and bearing the wrong kinds of leaves. For a while our view to the left was cut off by a fantastically woven fence of immense bramble trunks with spines as big as shovels. In another place a stretch of ground looked like a dried out riverbed full of large pebbles, but the pebbles turned out to be globular fungi set as close together as they could grow. There were trees with trunks too soft to stand upright so that they looped over and grew along the ground. Here and there were patches of miniature trees, shrunk and gnarled, and looking centuries old.

I glanced surreptitiously again at the man in the other pannier. There didn't seem to be anything wrong with him except that he was very dirty, as were his ragged clothes and crumpled hat. He caught my eye on him.

"Never been in the Fringes before, boy?" he asked.

"No," I told him. "Is it all like this?"

He grinned, and shook his head.

"None of it's like any other part. That's why the Fringes is the Fringes; pretty near nothing grows true to stock here, yet."

"Yet?" I repeated.

"Sure. It'll settle down though, in time. Wild Country was Fringes once, but it's steadier now; likely the parts you come from were Wild Country once, but they've settled down more. God's little game of patience I reckon it is, but he certainly takes his time over it."

"God?" I said doubtfully. "They've always taught us that it's the Devil that rules in the Fringes."

He shook his head.

"That's what they tell you over there. 'Tisn't so, boy. It's your parts where the old Devil's hanging on and looking after his own. Arrogant, they are. The true image, and all. . . . Want to be like the Old People. Tribulation hasn't taught 'em a thing. . . .

"The Old People thought *they* were the tops, too. Had ideals, they did; knew just how the world ought to be run. All they had to do was get it fixed up comfortable, and keep it that way, then everybody'd be fine, on account of their ideas being a lot more civilized than God's."

He shook his head.

"Didn't work out, boy. Couldn't work out. They weren't God's last word like they thought. God doesn't have any last word. If he did he'd be dead. But he isn't dead; and he changes and grows, like everything else that's alive. So when they were doing their best to get everything fixed and tidy on some kind of eternal lines they'd thought up for themselves, he sent along Tribulation to bust it up and remind 'em that life is change.

"He saw it wasn't going to come out the way things lay, so he shuffled the pack to see if it wouldn't give a better break next time."

He paused to consider that a moment, and went on:

"Maybe he didn't shuffle quite enough. The same sequences seem to have got kind of stuck together some places. Parts where you come from, for instance. There they are, still on the same lines, still reckoning they're the last word, still trying their damnedest to stay as they are and fix up just the same state of affairs that brought Tribulation last time. One day He's going to get pretty tired of the way they can't learn a lesson, and start showing them another trick or two."

"Oh," I said, vaguely, but safely. It was odd, I felt, how many people seemed to have positive, if conflicting, information upon God's views.

The man did not seem altogether satisfied that he had got his point home. He waved his hand at the deviational landscape about us, and I suddenly noticed his own irregularity—the right hand lacked the first three fingers.

"Some day," he proclaimed, "something is going to steady down out of all this. It'll be new, and new kinds of plants mean new creatures. Tribulation was a shake-up to give us a new start."

"But where they can make the stock breed true, they destroy Deviations," I pointed out.

"They try to, they think they do," he agreed. "They're pigheadedly determined to keep the Old People's standards. But do they? Can they? How do they *know* that their crops and their fruit and their vegetables are just the same? Aren't there disputes? And doesn't it nearly always turn out that the breed with the higher yield is accepted in the end? Aren't cattle cross-bred to get hardiness, or milk-yield, or meat? Sure, they can wipe out the obvious Deviations, but are you sure that the Old People would recognize any of the present breeds at all? I'm not, by any means. You can't stop it, you see. You can be obstructive and destructive, and you can slow it all up and distort it for your own ends, but somehow it just keeps on happening. Just look at these horses."

"They're government-approved," I told him.

"Sure. That's just what I mean," he said.

"But if it keeps on anyway, I don't see why there had to be Tribulation," I objected.

"For other forms it keeps on changing," he said, "but not for man, not for kinds like the Old People and your people, if they can help it. They stamp on any change. They close the way and keep the type fixed because they've got the arrogance to think themselves perfect. As they reckon it, they and only they are the true image; very well, then it follows that if the image *is* true, they themselves must be God, and being God they reckon themselves entitled to decree, 'thus far, and no farther.' That is their great sin: they try to strangle the life out of Life."

There was an air about the last few sentences, rather out of keeping with the rest, which caused me to suspect I had encountered some kind of creed once more. I decided to shift the conversation on to a more practical plane by inquiring why we had been taken prisoner.

He did not seem very sure about that, except to assure me

that it was always done when any stranger was found entering Fringes territory.

I thought that over, and then got into touch with Michael again.

"What do you suggest we tell them?" I asked. "I imagine there'll be an examination. When they find we're physically normal we shall have to give some reason for being on the run."

"Best to tell them the truth, only minimize it. Play it right down the way Katherine and Sally did. Just let them know enough to account for it," he suggested.

"Very well," I agreed. "Do you understand that, Petra? You tell them you can just make think-pictures to Rosalind and me. Nothing about Michael, or Zealand people."

"The Zealand people are coming to help. They're not so far away as they were, now," she told us confidently

Michael received that with skepticism. "All very nice—*if* they can. But don't mention them."

"All right," Petra agreed.

We discussed whether we would tell our two guards about the intended pursuit, and decided it would do no harm

The man in the other pannier showed no surprise at the news.

"Good. That'll suit us," he said. But he explained no further, and we plodded steadily on.

Petra began to converse with her distant friend again, and there was no doubt that the distance was less. Petra did not have to use such disturbing force to reach her, and for the first time I was able by straining hard to catch bits of the other side of the exchange. Rosalind caught it, too. She put out a question as strongly as she could. The unknown strengthened her projection and came to us clearly, pleased to have made contact, and anxious to know more than Petra could tell.

Rosalind explained what she could of our present situation, and that we did not seem to be in immediate danger. The other advised:

"Be cautious. Agree to whatever they say, and play for time Be emphatic about the danger you are in from your own people. It is difficult to advise you without knowing the tribe

Some deviational tribes detest the appearance of normality. It can't do any harm to exaggerate how different you are *inside* from your own people. The really important matter is the little girl. Keep her safe at all costs. We have never before known such a power of projection in one so young. What is her name?"

Rosalind spelled it out in letter forms. Then she asked:

"But who are you? What is this Zealand?"

"We are the New People—your kind of people. The people who can think-together. We're the people who are going to build a new kind of world—different from the Old People's world, and from the savages'."

"The kind of people that God intended, perhaps?" I inquired, with a feeling of being on familiar ground again.

"I don't know about that. Who does? But we do know that we can make a better world than the Old People did. They were only ingenious half-humans, little better than savages; all living shut off from one another, with only clumsy words to link them. Emotions they could sometimes share, but they could not think collectively. When their conditions were primitive they could get along all right, as the animals can; but the more complex they made their world, the less capable they were of dealing with it. They had no means of consensus. They learnt to cooperate constructively in small units; but only destructively in large units. They aspired greedily, and then refused to face the responsibilities they had created. They created vast problems, and then buried their heads in the sands of idle faith. There was, you see, no real communication, no understanding between them. They could, at their best, be near-sublime animals, but not more.

"They could never have succeeded. If they had not brought down Tribulation which all but destroyed them, then they would have bred with the carelessnes of animals until they had reduced themselves to poverty and misery, and ultimately to starvation and barbarism. One way or another they were foredoomed because they were an inadequate species."

It occurred to me again that these Zealanders had no little opinion of themselves. To one brought up as I had been this irreverence for the Old People was difficult to take. While I was still wrestling with it Rosalind asked:

"But you? Where do you come from?"

"Our ancestors had the good fortune to live on an island—or, rather, two islands—somewhat secluded. They did not escape Tribulation and its effects even there, though it was less violent there than in most places, but they were cut off from the rest of the world, and sank back almost to barbarism. Then, somehow, the strain of people who could think-together began. In time, those who were able to do it best found others who could do it a little, and taught them to develop it. It was natural for the people who could share thoughts to tend to marry one another, so that the strain was strengthened.

"Later on, they started to discover thought-shape makers in other places, too. That was when they began to understand how fortunate they had been; they found that even in places where physical deviations don't count for much people who have think-together are usually persecuted.

"For a long time nothing could be done to help the same kind of people in other places—though some tried to sail to Zealand in canoes, and sometimes they got there—but later, when we had machines again, we were able to fetch some of them to safety. Now we try to do that whenever we make contact, but we have never before made contact at anything like this distance. It is still a strain for me to reach you. It will get easier, but I shall have to stop now. Look after the little girl. She is unique and tremendously important. Protect her at all costs."

The thought patterns faded away, leaving nothing for a moment. Then Petra came in. Whatever she may have failed to make of the rest, she had caught the last part all right.

"That's me," she proclaimed, with satisfaction and totally unnecessary vigor.

We rocked, and recovered.

"Beware, odious smug child. We haven't met Hairy Jack yet," Rosalind told her, with subduing effect. "Michael," she added, "did all that reach you, too?"

"Yes," Michael responded with a touch of reserve. "Condescending, I thought. Sounded as if she were lecturing to children. Still coming from a devil of a long way away, too. I don't see how they can come fast enough to be any help at all. We shall be starting after you in a few minutes now."

The greathorses clumped steadily on. The landscape was disturbing and alarming to one brought up in respect for the property of forms. Certainly, few things were as fantastic as the growths that Uncle Axel had told of in the South; on the other hand, practically nothing was comfortably familiar, or even orthodox. There was so much confusion that it did not seem to matter any more whether a particular tree was an aberrate or just a miscegenate, but it was a relief to get away from trees and out into open country for a bit, though even there the bushes weren't homogeneal or identifiable, and the grass was pretty queer, too.

We stopped only once for food and drink, and for no more than half an hour before we were on our way again. Two hours or so later, after several more stretches of woodlands, we reached a medium-sized river. On our side the level ground descended in a sharp, steep bank to the water; on the other stood a line of low, reddish cliffs.

We turned downstream, keeping along the top of the bank. A quarter of a mile along, at a place marked by a grossly deviational tree shaped like a huge wooden pear, and with all its branches growing in one big tuft at the top, a runnel cut well back into the bank and made a way for the horses to get down. We forded the river obliquely, making for a gap in the opposite cliffs. When we reached it, it turned out to be little more than a cleft, so narrow in some places that the panniers scraped both walls, and we could scarcely squeeze through. There was quite a hundred yards of it before the way widened and began to slope up to normal ground level.

Where the sides diminished to mere banks, seven or eight men stood with bows in their hands. They gaped incredulously at the greathorses, and looked half-inclined to run. Abreast of them, we stopped.

The man in the other pannier scrambled on to the saddle and leaned down to cut the cord on my wrists with a long knife.

"Down you get, boy," he told me.

Petra and Rosalind were already climbing down from the leading greathorse. As I reached the ground the driver gave a thump and both greathorses moved on with stately ponderousness. Petra clasped my hand nervously, but for the moment all the ragged, unkempt bowmen were still more interested in the horses than in us.

There was nothing immediately alarming about the group. One of the hands which held a bow had six fingers; one man displayed a head like a polished brown egg, without a hair on it, or on his face; another had immensely large feet and hands; but whatever was wrong with the rest was hidden under their rags.

Rosalind and I shared a feeling of relief at not being confronted with the kinds of grotesquerie we had half-expected. Petra, too, was encouraged to find that none of them fulfilled the traditional description of Hairy Jack. Presently, when they had watched the horses out of sight up a track that disappeared among trees, they turned their attention to us. A couple of them told us to come along, the rest remained where they were.

A well-used path led downward through woods for a few hundred yards, and then gave on to a clearing. On the right ran a wall of the reddish cliffs again, not more than forty feet high. They appeared to be the reverse side of the ridge which retained the river, and the whole face was pocked by numerous holes, with ladders, roughly made of branches, leading to the higher openings.

The level ground in front was littered with crude huts and tents. One or two small cooking fires smoked among them. A few tattered men and a rather larger number of slatternly-looking women moved around with no great activity.

We wound our way among hovels and refuse-heaps until we reached the largest of the tents. It appeared to be an old rick-cover—the loot, presumably, of some raid—fastened over a framework of lashed poles. A figure seated on a stool just inside the entrance looked up as we approached. The sight of his face jolted me with panic for a moment—it was so like my father's. Then I recognized him—the same "spider-man" I had seen as a captive at Waknuk, seven or eight years before.

The two men who had brought us pushed us forward, in front of him. He looked the three of us over. His eyes traveled up and down Rosalind's slim straight figure in a way I did not care for—nor she, either. Then he studied me more carefully, and nodded to himself, as if satisfied over something.

"Remember me?" he asked.

"Yes," I told him.

He shifted his gaze from my face. He let it stray over the conglomeration of hutches and shacks, and then back again to me.

"Not much like Waknuk," he said.

"Not much," I agreed.

He paused quite lengthily, in contemplation. Then:

"Know who I am?" he inquired.

"I think so. I think I found out," I told him.

He raised an eyebrow, questioningly.

"My father had an elder brother," I said. "He was thought to be normal until he was about three or four years old. Then his certificate was revoked, and he was sent away."

He nodded slowly.

"But not *quite* right," he said. "His mother loved him. His nurse was fond of him, too. So when they came to take him away he was already missing—but they'd hush that up, of course. They'd hush the whole thing up, pretend it never happened." He paused again, reflectively. Presently he added, "The eldest son. The heir. Waknuk should be mine. It would be, except for *this*." He stretched out his long arm, and regarded it for a moment. Then he dropped it and looked at me again.

"Do you know what the length of a man's arm should be?"

"No," I admitted.

"Nor do I. But somebody in Rigo does, some expert on the true image. So, no Waknuk, and I must live like a savage among savages. Are you the eldest son?"

"The only son," I told him. "There was a younger one, but——"

"No certificate, eh?"

I nodded.

"So you, too, have lost Waknuk!"

That aspect of things had never troubled me. I do not think I had ever had any real expectation of inheriting Waknuk. There had always been the sense of insecurity, the expectation, almost the certainty, that one day I should be discovered. I had lived too long with that expectation to feel the resentment that embittered him. Now that it was resolved, I was glad to be safely away, and I told him so. It did not please him. He looked at me thoughtfully.

"You've not the guts to fight for what's yours by right?" he suggested.

"If it's yours by right, it can't be mine by right," I pointed out. "But my meaning was that I've had more than enough of living in hiding."

"We all live in hiding here," he said.

"Maybe," I told him. "But you can be your own selves. You don't have to live a pretense. You don't have to watch yourselves every moment, and think twice whenever you open your mouths."

He nodded slowly.

"We heard about you. We have our ways," he said. "What I don't understand is why they are after you in such strength."

"We think," I explained, "that we worry them more than the usual deviants because they've no way of identifying us. I fancy they must be suspecting that there are a lot more of us that they haven't discovered, and they want to get hold of us to make us tell."

"An even more than usually good reason for not being caught," he said.

I was aware that Michael had come in and that Rosalind was answering him, but I could not attend to two conversations at once, so I left that to her.

"So they are coming right into the Fringes after you? How many of them?" he asked.

"I'm not sure," I said, considering how to play our hand to the best advantage.

"From what I've heard, you should have ways of finding out," he said.

I wondered how much he did know about us, and whether he knew about Michael, too, but that seemed unlikely. With his eyes a little narrowed, he went on:

"It'll be better not to fool with us, boy. It's you they're after, and you've brought trouble this way with you. Why should we care what happens to you? Quite easy to put one of you where they'd find you."

Petra caught the implication of that, and panicked.

"More than a hundred men," she said.

He turned a thoughtful eye on her for a moment.

"So there *is* one of you with them—I rather thought there might be," he observed, and nodded again. "A hundred men is a great many to send after just you three. Too many. . . . I see. . . ." He turned back to me. "There will have been rumors lately about trouble working up in the Fringes?"

"Yes," I admitted.

He grinned.

"So it comes in handy. For the first time they decide that they will take the initiative, and invade us—and pick you up, too, of course. They'll be following your trail, naturally. How far have they got?"

I consulted Michael, and learned that the main body had still some miles to go before they would join the party that had fired on us and bolted the greathorses. The difficulty then was to find a way of conveying the position intelligently to the man in front of me. He appreciated that, and did not seem greatly perturbed.

"Is your father with them?" he asked.

That was a question which I had been careful not to put to Michael before. I did not put it now. I simply paused for a moment, and then told him "No." Out of the corner of my eye I noticed Petra about to speak and felt Rosalind pounce on her.

"A pity," said the spidery man. "It's quite a time now I've been hoping that one day I'd meet your father on equal terms. From what I've heard I should have thought he'd be there. Maybe he's not such a valiant champion of the true image as they say." He went on looking at me with a steady, penetrating gaze. I could feel Rosalind's sympathy, her understanding why I had not put the question to Michael, like a handclasp.

Then, quite suddenly, the man dismissed me from his attention and turned to consider Rosalind. She looked back at him. She stood with her straight, confident air, eyeing him levelly and coldly for long seconds. Then, suddenly, to my astonishment, she broke. Her eyes dropped. She flushed. He smiled slightly.

But he was wrong. It was not surrender to the stronger character, the conqueror. It was loathing, a horror which broke her defenses from within. I had a glimpse of him from her mind, hideously exaggerated. The fears she hid so well burst up and she was terrified; not as a woman weakened by a man, but as a child in terror of a monstrosity. Petra, too, caught the involuntary shape, and it shocked her into a scream.

I jumped full at the man, overturning the stool and sending him sprawling. The two men behind us leaped after me, but I got in at least one good blow before they could drag me off.

The spider-man sat up, and rubbed his jaw. He grinned at me, but not with any amusement.

"Does you credit," he conceded, "but not much more." He got up on his gangling legs. "Not seen much of the women around here, have you, boy? Take a look at 'em as you go. Maybe you'll understand a bit more. Besides, this one can have children. I've had a fancy for some children a long time now, even if they do happen to take after their father a bit." He grinned briefly again, and then frowned at us. "Better take it the way it is, boy. Be a sensible fellow. I don't give second chances."

He looked from me to the men who were holding me.

"Chuck him out," he told them. "And if he doesn't seem to understand that that means stay out, shoot him."

The two of them jerked me round and marched me off. At the edge of the clearing one of them helped me along a path with his boot.

"Keep on going," he said.

I got up and turned around, but one of them had an arrow trained on me. He gave a shake of his head to urge me on. So I did what I was told, kept on going—for a few yards, until the trees hid me. Then I doubled back under cover.

Just what they were expecting. But they didn't shoot me; they just beat me up and slung me back among the undergrowth. I remember flying through the air, but I don't remember landing. . . .

Chapter Fifteen

I WAS BEING DRAGGED ALONG. There were hands under my shoulders. Small branches were whipping back and slapping me in the face.

"What——?" I began.

"Sh!" whispered a voice behind me.

"Give me a minute. I'll be all right," I whispered back.

The dragging stopped. I lay pulling myself together for a moment, and then rolled over. A woman, a young woman, was sitting back on her heels, looking at me.

The sun was low now, and it was dim under the trees. I could not see her well. There was dark hair hanging down on each side of a sunburnt face, and the glint of dark eyes regarding me earnestly. The bodice of her dress was ragged, a nondescript tawny color, with stains on it. There were no sleeves, but what struck me most was that it bore no cross. I had never before been face to face with a woman who wore no protective cross stitched to her dress. It looked queer, almost indecent. We faced one another for some seconds.

"You don't know me, David," she said sadly.

Until then I had not. It was the way she said "David" that suddenly told me.

"Sophie!" I said, "Oh, Sophie!"

She smiled.

"Dear David," she said. "Have they hurt you badly, David?"

I tried moving my arms and legs. They were stiff and they ached in several places, so did my body and my head. I felt some blood caked on my left cheek, but there seemed to be nothing broken. I started to get up, but she stretched out a hand and put it on my arm.

"No, not yet. Wait a little, till it's dark." She went on looking at me. "I saw them bring you in. You and the little girl, and the other girl. Who is she, David?"

That brought me fully round, with a jolt. Frantically I sought for Rosalind and Petra, and could not reach them. Michael felt my panic and came in steadyingly. Relieved, too.

"Thank goodness for that. We've been worried stiff about you. Take it easy. They're all right, both of them tired out and exhausted; they've fallen asleep."

"Is Rosalind——?"

"She's all right, I tell you. What's been happening to you?"

I told him. The whole exchange only took a few seconds, but long enough for Sophie to be regarding me curiously.

"Who is she, David?" she repeated.

I explained that Rosalind was my cousin. She watched me as I spoke, and then nodded slowly.

"*He* wants her, doesn't he?" she asked.

"That's what he said," I admitted, grimly.

"She could give him babies?" she persisted.

"What are you trying to do to me?" I asked her.

"So, you're in love with her?" she went on.

A word again. . . . When the minds have learned to mingle, when no thought is wholly one's own, and each has taken too much of the other ever to be entirely himself alone; when one has reached the beginning of seeing with a single eye, loving with a single heart, enjoying with a single joy; when there can be moments of identity and nothing is separate save bodies that long for one another. . . . When there is that, where is the word? There is only the inadequacy of the word that exists.

"We love one another," I said.

Sophie nodded. She picked up a few twigs, and watched her brown fingers break them. She said:

"He's gone away—where the fighting is. She's safe just now."

"She's asleep," I told her. "They're both asleep."

Her eyes came back to mine, puzzled.

"How do you know?"

I told her briefly, as simply as I could. She went on breaking twigs as she listened. Then she nodded.

"I remember. My mother said there was something . . .

something about the way you sometimes seemed to understand her before she spoke. Was that it?"

"I think so. I think your mother had a little of it, without knowing she had it," I said.

"It must be a very wonderful thing to have," she said, half wistfully. "Like more eyes, inside you."

"Something like," I admitted. "It's difficult to explain. But it isn't all wonderful. It can hurt a lot sometimes."

"To be any kind of deviant is to be hurt—always," she said. She continued to sit back on her heels, looking at her hands in her lap, seeing nothing.

"If she were to give him children, he wouldn't want me any more," she said, at last.

There was still enough light to catch a glistening on her cheeks.

"Sophie, dear," I said. "Are you in love with him—with this spider-man?"

"Oh, don't call him that—please—we can't any of us help being what we are. His name's Gordon. He's kind to me, David. He's fond of me. You've got to have as little as I have to know how much that means. You've never known loneliness. You can't understand the awful emptiness that's waiting all around us here. I'd have given him babies gladly, if I could. I—oh, why do they do that to us? Why didn't they kill me? It would have been kinder than this."

She sat without a sound. The tears squeezed out from under the closed lids and ran down her face. I took her hand between my own.

I remembered watching. The man with his arm linked in the woman's, the small figure on top of the packhorse waving back to me as they disappeared into the trees. Myself desolate, a kiss still damp on my cheek, a lock tied with a yellow ribbon in my hand. I looked at her now, and my heart ached.

"Sophie," I said. "Sophie, darling. It's not going to happen. Do you understand? It won't happen. Rosalind will never let it happen. I *know* that."

She opened her eyes again, and looked at me through the brimming tears.

"You can't *know* a thing like that about another person. You're just trying to——"

"I'm not, Sophie. I do know. You and I could only *know* very little about one another. But with Rosalind it is different: it's part of what thinking-together means."

She regarded me doubtfully.

"Is that really true? I don't understand."

"How should you? But it *is* true. I could feel what she was feeling about the spi—about that man."

She went on looking at me, a trifle uneasily.

"You can't see what I think?" she inquired, with a touch of anxiety.

"No more than you can tell what I think," I assured her. "It isn't a kind of spying. It's more as if you could just talk all your thoughts, if you liked—and not talk them if you wanted them private."

It was more difficult trying to explain it to her than it had been to Uncle Axel, but I kept on struggling to simplify it into words until I suddenly became aware that the light had gone, and I was talking to a figure I could scarcely see. I broke off.

"Is it dark enough now?"

"Yes. It'll be safe if we go carefully," she told me. "Can you walk all right? It isn't far."

I got up, well aware of stiffness and bruises, but not of anything worse. She seemed able to see better in the gloom than I could, and took my hand, to lead the way. We kept to the trees, but I could see fires twinkling on my left, and realized that we were skirting the encampment. We kept on round it until we reached the low cliff that closed the northwest side, and then along the base of that, in the shadow, for fifty yards or so. There she stopped, and laid my hand on one of the rough ladders I had seen against the rock face.

"Follow me," she whispered, and suddenly whisked upward.

I climbed more cautiously until I reached the top of the ladder where it rested against a rock ledge. Her arm reached out and helped me in.

"Sit down," she told me.

The lighter patch through which I had come disappeared. She moved about, looking for something. Presently there were sparks as she used a flint and steel. She blew up the sparks until she was able to light a pair of candles. They were short, fat, burnt with smoky flames, and smelled abominable, but they enabled me to see the surroundings.

The place was a cave about fifteen feet deep and nine wide, cut out of the sandy rock. The entrance was covered by a skin curtain hooked across it. In one corner of the inner end there was a flaw in the roof from which water dripped steadily at about a drop a second. It fell into a wooden bucket; the overflow of the bucket trickled down a groove for the full length of the cave, and out of the entrance. In the other inner corner was a mattress of small branches, with skins and a tattered blanket on it. There were a few bowls and utensils. A blackened fire-hollow near the entrance, empty now, showed an ingenious draft-hole drilled to the outer air. The handles of a few knives and other tools protruded from niches in the walls. A spear, a bow, a leather quiver with a dozen arrows in it, lay close to the brushwood mattress. There was nothing much else.

I thought of the kitchen of the Wenders' cottage. The clean, bright room that had seemed so friendly because it had no texts on the walls. The candles flickered, sent greasy smoke up to the roof, and stank.

Sophie dipped a bowl into the bucket, rummaged a fairly clean bit of rag out of a niche, and brought it across to me. She washed the blood off my face and out of my hair, and examined the cause.

"Just a cut. Not deep," she said, reassuringly.

I washed my hands in the bowl. She tipped the water into the runnel, rinsed the bowl and put it away.

"You're hungry, David?" she said.

"Very," I told her. I had had nothing to eat all day except during our one brief stop.

"Stay here. I won't be long," she instructed, and slipped out under the skin curtain.

I sat looking at the shadows that danced on the rock walls, listening to the plop-plop-plop of the drips. And very likely, I told myself, this is luxury, in the Fringes. "You've got to have as little as I have——" Sophie had said, though it had not been material things that she meant. To escape the forlorn-ness and the squalor I sought Michael's company.

"Where are you? What's been happening?" I asked him.

"We've camped for the night," he told me. "Too dangerous to go on in the dark." He tried to give me a picture of the place as he had seen it just before sunset, but it might have been a dozen spots along our route. "It's been slow going all day—tiring, too. They know their woods, these Fringes people. We've been expecting a real ambush somewhere on the way, but it's been sniping and harassing all the time. We've lost three killed, but had seven wounded—only two of them seriously."

"But you're still coming on?"

"Yes. The feeling is that now we do have quite a force here for once, it's a chance to give the Fringes something that will keep them quiet for some time to come. Besides, you three are badly wanted. There's a rumor that there are a couple of dozen, perhaps more, of us scattered about Waknuk and surrounding districts, and you have to be brought back to identify them." He paused a moment there, then he went on in a worried, unhappy mood.

"In point of fact, David, I'm afraid—very much afraid—there is only one."

"One?"

"Deborah managed to reach me, right at her limit, very faintly. She says something has happened to Mark."

"They've caught him?"

"No. She thinks not. He'd have let her know if it were that. He's simply stopped. Not a thing from him in over twenty-four hours now."

"An accident perhaps? Remember Walter Brent—that boy who was killed by a tree? He just stopped like that."

"It might be. Deborah just doesn't know. She's frightened; it leaves her all alone now. She was right at her limit, and I was almost. Another two or three miles, and we'll be out of touch."

"It's queer I didn't hear at least your side of this," I told him.

"Probably while you were knocked out," he suggested.

"Well, when Petra wakes she'll be able to keep touch with Deborah," I reminded him. "She doesn't seem to have any kind of limit."

"Yes, of course. I'd forgotten that," he agreed. "It will help her a bit."

A few moments later a hand came under the curtain, pushing a wooden bowl into the cave mouth. Sophie scrambled in after it, and gave it to me. She trimmed up the disgusting candles and then squatted down on the skin of some unidentifiable animal while I helped myself with a wooden spoon. An odd dish; it appeared to consist of several kinds of shoots, diced meat, and crumbled hard-bread, but the result was not at all bad, and very welcome. I enjoyed it, almost to the last, when I was suddenly smitten in a way that sent a whole spoonful cascading down my shirt. Petra was awake again.

I got in a response at once. Petra switched straight from distress to elation. It was flattering, but almost as painful. Evidently she woke Rosalind, for I caught her pattern among the chaos of Michael asking what the hell? and Petra's Zealand friend anxiously protesting.

Presently Petra got a hold of herself, and the turmoil quietened down. There was a sense of all other parties relaxing cautiously.

"Is she safe now? What was all that thunder and lightning about?" Michael inquired.

Petra told us, keeping it down with an obvious effort; "We thought David was dead. We thought they'd killed him."

Now I began to catch Rosalind's thoughts, firming into comprehensible shapes out of a sort of swirl. I was humbled, bowled over, happy, and distressed all at the same time. I could not think much more clearly in response, for all I tried. It was Michael who put an end to that.

"This is scarcely decent for third parties," he observed. "When you two can disentangle yourselves, there are other things to be discussed." He paused. "Now," he continued, "what is the position?"

We sorted it out. Rosalind and Petra were still in the tent where I had last seen them. The spider-man had gone away, leaving a large, pink-eyed, white-haired man in charge of them. I explained my situation.

"Very well," said Michael. "You say this spider-man seems to be in some sort of authority, and that he has come forward toward the fighting. You've no idea whether he intends to join in the fighting himself, or whether he is simply making tactical dispositions? You see, if it is the latter he may come back at any time."

"I've no idea," I told him.

Rosalind came in abruptly, as near to hysteria as I had known her.

"I'm frightened of him. He's a different kind. Not like us. Not the same sort at all. It would be outrageous—like an animal. I couldn't, ever . . . if he tries to take me I shall kill myself. . . ."

Michael threw himself on that like a pail of ice-water.

"You won't do anything so damned silly. You'll kill the spider-man, if necessary." With an air of having settled that point conclusively he turned his attention elsewhere. At his full range he directed a question at Petra's friend.

"You still think you can reach us?"

The reply came still from a long distance, but clearly and without effort now. It was a calmly confident "Yes."

"When?" Michael asked.

There was a pause before the reply, as if for consultation, then:

"In not more than sixteen hours from now," she told him, just as confidently. Michael's skepticism diminished. For the first time he allowed himself to admit the possibility of her help.

"Then it is a question of insuring that you three are kept safe for that long," he told us, meditatively.

"Wait a minute. Just hold on a bit," I told them.

I looked up at Sophie. The smoky candles gave enough light to show that she was watching my face intently, a little uneasily.

"You were 'talking' to that girl?" she said.

"And my sister. They're awake now," I told her. "They are in the tent, and being guarded by an albino. It seems odd."

"Odd?" she inquired.

"Well, one would have thought a woman in charge of them. . . ."

"This is the Fringes," she reminded me, with bitterness.

"It—oh, I see," I said, awkwardly. "Well, the point is this: do you think there is any way they can be got out of there before he comes back? It seems to me that now is the time.

Once he does come back. . . ." I shrugged, keeping my eyes on hers.

She turned her head away and contemplated the candles for some moments. Then she nodded.

"Yes. That would be best for all of us—all of us, except him," she added, half-sadly. "Yes, I think it can be done."

"Straight away?"

She nodded again. I picked up the spear that lay by the couch, and weighed it in my hand. It was somewhat light, but well balanced. She looked at it, and shook her head.

"You must stay here, David," she told me.

"But——" I began.

"No. If you were to be seen, there would be an alarm. No one will take any notice of me going to his tent, even if they do see me."

There was sense in that. I laid the spear down, though with reluctance.

"But can you——?"

"Yes," she said, decisively.

She got up and went to one of the niches. From it she pulled out a knife. The broad blade was clean and bright. It looked as if it might once have been part of the kitchen furnishings of a raided farm. She slipped it into the belt of her skirt, leaving only the dark handle protruding. Then she turned and looked at me for a long moment.

"David——" she began, tentatively.

"What?" I asked.

She changed her mind. In a different tone she said, "Will you tell them no noise? Whatever happens, no sounds at all? Tell them to follow me, and have dark pieces of cloth ready to wrap around themselves. Will you be able to make all that clear to them?"

"Yes," I told her. "But I wish you'd let me——"

She shook her head and cut me short.

"No, David. It'd only increase the risk. You don't know the place."

She pinched out the candles, and unhooked the curtain. For a moment I saw her silhouetted against the paler darkness of the entrance, then she was gone.

I gave her instructions to Rosalind, and we impressed on

Petra the necessity for silence. Then there was nothing to do but wait and listen to the steady drip-drip-drip in the darkness.

I could not sit still for long like that. I went to the entrance and put my head out into the night. There were a few cooking fires glowing among the shades, people moving about, too, for the glows blinked occasionally as figures crossed in front of them. There was a murmur of voices, a slight, composite stir of small movements, a night-bird calling harshly a little distance away, the cry of an animal still farther off. Nothing more.

We were all waiting. A small shapeless surge of excitement escaped for a moment from Petra. No one commented on it.

Then from Rosalind a reassuring, "it's-all-right" shape, but with a curious secondary quality of shock to it. It seemed wiser not to distract their attention now by asking about it.

I listened. There was no alarm, no change in the conglomerate murmur. It seemed a long time until I heard the crunch of grit underfoot directly below me. The poles of the ladder scraped faintly on the rock edge as the weight came on them. I moved back into the cave out of the way. Rosalind was asking silently, a little doubtfully:

"Is this right? Are you there, David?"

"Yes. Come along up," I told them.

One figure appeared dimly outlined in the opening. Then another, smaller form, then a third. The opening was blotted out. Presently the candles were alight again.

Rosalind, and Petra, too, watched silently in horrid fascination as Sophie scooped a bowlful of water from the bucket to wash the blood off her arms and clean the knife.

Chapter Sixteen

THE TWO GIRLS studied one another, curiously and warily. Sophie's eyes traveled over Rosalind, in her russet woolen dress with its brown cross applique, and rested anxiously for a moment on her leather shoes. She looked down at her own soft moccasins, then at her short, tattered skirt. In the course of her self-inspection she discovered new stains that had not been on her bodice half an hour before. Without any embarrassment she pulled it off and began to soak them out in the cold water. To Rosalind she said:

"You must get rid of that cross. Hers, as well," she added glancing at Petra. "It marks you. We women in the Fringes do not feel that it has served us very well. The men resent it, too. Here." She took a small, thin-bladed knife from a niche, and held it out.

Rosalind took it, doubtfully. She looked at it, and then down at the cross which had been displayed on every dress she had ever worn. Sophie watched her.

"I used to wear one," she said. "It didn't help me, either."

Rosalind looked at me, still a little doubtfully. I nodded.

"They don't much like insistence on the true image in these parts. Very likely it's dangerous." I glanced at Sophie.

"It is," she said. "It's not only an identification; it's a challenge."

Rosalind lifted the knife and began, half-reluctantly, to pick at the stitches.

I said to Sophie: "What now? Oughtn't we to try to get as far away as we can before it's light?"

Sophie, still dabbling her bodice, shook her head.

"No. They may find him any time. When they do, there'll be a search. They'll think that you killed him and then all three of you took to the woods. They'll never think of looking for you here, why should they? But they'll rake the whole neighborhood for you."

"You mean, we stay here?" I asked her. She nodded.

"For two, perhaps three days. Then, when they've called off the search, I'll see you clear."

Rosalind looked up from her unpicking thoughtfully.

"Why are you doing all this for us?" she asked.

I explained to her about Sophie and the spider-man far more quickly than it could have been put into words. It did not seem to satisfy her entirely. She and Sophie went on regarding one another steadily in the flickering light.

Sophie dropped the bodice into the water with a plop. She stood up slowly. She bent toward Rosalind, locks of dark hair dangling down on her naked breasts, her eyes narrowed.

"Damn you," she said viciously. "Leave me alone, damn you."

Rosalind became taut, ready for any movement. I shifted so that I could jump between them if necessary. The tableau held for long seconds. Sophie, uncared for, half-naked in her ragged skirt, dangerously poised; Rosalind, in her brown dress with the unpicked left arm of the cross hanging forward, with her bronze hair shining in the candlelight, her fine features upturned, with eyes alert. The crisis passed, and the tension lost pitch. The violence died out of Sophie's eyes, but she did not move. Her mouth twisted a little and she trembled.

"Damn you!" she said again. "Go on, laugh at me. Laugh at me because I *do* want him, *me!*" She gave a queer, choked laugh herself. "And what's the use? Oh, God, what's the use? If he weren't in love with you, what good would I be to him—like this?"

She clenched her hands to her face and stood for a moment, shaking all over, then she turned and flung herself on the brushwood bed.

We stared into the shadowy corner. One moccasin had fallen off. I could see the brown, grubby sole of her foot, and the line of six toes. I turned to Rosalind. Her eyes met mine, contrite and appalled. Instinctively she made to get up. I shook my head, and, hesitantly she sank back.

The only sounds in the cave were the hopeless, abandoned sobbing, and plop-plop-plop of the drips.

Petra looked at us, then at the figure on the bed, then at us again, expectantly. When neither of us moved she appeared to decide that the initiative lay with her. She crossed to the bedside and knelt down concernedly beside it. Tentatively she put a hand on the dark hair.

"Don't," she said. "Please *don't*."

There was a startled catch in the sobbing. A pause, then a brown arm reached out around Petra's shoulders. The sound became a little less desolate . . . it no longer tore at one's heart; but it left it bruised and aching. . . .

I awoke reluctantly, stiff and cold from lying on the hard rock floor. Almost immediately there was Michael:

"Did you mean to sleep all day?"

I looked up and saw a chink of daylight beneath the skin curtain.

"What's the time?" I asked him.

"About eight, I'd guess. It's been light for three hours, and we've fought a battle already."

"What happened?" I inquired.

"We got wind of an ambush, so we sent an outflanking party. It clashed with the reserve force that was waiting to follow up the ambush. Apparently they thought it was our main body; anyway, the result was a rout, at a cost of two or three wounded, to us."

"So now you're coming on?"

"Yes. I suppose they'll rally somewhere, but they've melted away now. No opposition at all."

That was by no means as one could have wished. I explained our position, and that we certainly could not hope to emerge from the cave in daylight, unseen. On the other hand, if we stayed, and the place were to be captured, it would undoubtedly be searched, and we should be found.

"What about Petra's Zealand friends?" Michael asked. "Can you really count on them, do you think?"

Petra's friend, herself, came in on that, somewhat coolly.

"You *can* count on us."

"Your estimated time is the same? You've not been delayed?" Michael asked.

"Just the same," she assured us. "Approximately eight and a half hours from now." Then the slightly huffy note dropped, a tinge almost of awe colored her thoughts.

"This is a dreadful country indeed. We have seen Badlands before, but none of us has even imagined anything quite so terrible as this. There are stretches of miles across where it looks as if all the ground has been fused into black glass; there is nothing else, nothing but the glass like a frozen ocean of ink . . . then belts of Badlands . . . then another wilderness of black glass. It goes on and on. . . . What did they do here? What can they have done to create such a frightful place? No wonder none of us ever came this way before. It's like going over the rim of the world, into the outskirts of hell. It must be utterly beyond hope, barred to any kind of life for ever and ever . . . but why?—why?—why? There was the power of gods in the hands of children, we know; but were they *mad* children, all of them quite mad? . . . The mountains are cinders and the plains are black glass—still, after centuries! It is so dreary, dreary. A monstrous madness. . . . It is frightening to think that a whole race could go insane. If we did not know that you are on the other side of it we should have turned back and fled——"

Petra cut her off, abruptly blotting everything with distress. We had not known she was awake. I don't know what she had made of most of it, but she had clearly caught that thought of turning back. I went across to soothe her down, so that presently the Zealand woman was able to get through again and reassure her. The alarm subsided, and Petra recovered herself.

Michael came in, asking, "David, what about Deborah?"

I remembered his anxiety the previous night.

"Petra, darling," I said, "we've got too far away now for any of us to reach Deborah. Will you ask her something?"

Petra nodded.

"We want to know if she has heard anything of Mark since she talked to Michael."

Petra put the question. She shook her head.

"No," she said. "She hasn't heard anything. She's very

miserable, I think. She wants to know if Michael is all right."

"Tell her he's quite all right—we all are. Tell her we love her, we're terribly sorry she's all alone, but she must be brave—and careful. She must try not to let anyone see she's worried."

"She understands. She says she'll try," Petra reported. She remained thoughtful for a moment. Then she said to me, in words, "Deborah's afraid. She's crying inside. She wants Michael."

"Did she tell you that?" I asked.

Petra shook her head. "No. It was a sort of behind-think, but I saw it."

"We'd better not say anything about it," I decided. "It's not our business. A person's behind-thinks aren't really meant for other people, so we must just pretend not to have noticed them."

"All right," Petra agreed, equably.

I hoped it was all right. When I thought it over I wasn't at all sure that I cared much for this business of detecting "behind-thinks." It left one a trifle uneasy, and retrospective. . . .

Sophie woke up a few minutes later. She seemed calm, competent again, as though the last night's storm had blown itself out. She sent us to the back of the cave and unhooked the curtain to let the daylight in. Presently she had a fire going in the hollow. The greater part of the smoke from it went out of the entrance; the rest did at least have the compensation that it helped to obscure the interior of the cave from any outside observation. She ladled measures from two or three bags into an iron pot, added some water, and put the pot on the fire.

"Watch it," she instructed Rosalind, and then disappeared down the outside ladder.

Some twenty minutes later her head reappeared. She threw a couple of disks of hard bread over the sill and climbed in after them. She went to the pot, stirred it, and sniffed at the contents.

"No trouble?" I asked her.

"Not about that," she said. "They found him. They think you did it. There was a search—of a sort—early this morning. It wasn't as much of a search as it would have been with more men. But now they've got other things to worry about.

The men who went to the fighting are coming back in twos and threes. What happened, do you know?"

I told of the ambush that had failed, and the resulting disappearance of resistance.

"How far have they come now?" she wanted to know.

I inquired of Michael.

"We're just clear of forest for the first time, and into rough country," he told me.

I handed it on to Sophie. She nodded. "Three hours, or a bit less, perhaps, to the riverbank," she said.

She ladled the species of porridge out of the pot into bowls. It tasted better than it looked. The bread was less palatable. She broke a disk of it with a stone, and it had to be dipped in water before one could eat it. Petra grumbled that it was not proper food like we had at home. That reminded her of something. Without any warning she launched a question:

"Michael is my father there?"

It took him off guard. I caught his "yes" forming before he could suppress it.

I looked at Petra, hoping the implications were lost on her. Mercifully, they were. Rosalind lowered her bowl and stared into it silently.

Suspicion insulated one curiously little against the shock of knowledge. I could recall my father's voice, doctrinaire, relentless. I knew the expression his face would be wearing, as if I had seen him when he spoke.

"A baby—a baby which would grow to breed, and, breeding, spread pollution until all around us there would be Mutants and Abominations. That has happened in places where the will and faith were weak, but here it shall *never* happen."

And then my Aunt Harriet, "I shall pray God to send charity into this hideous world."

Poor Aunt Harriet, with her prayers as futile as her hopes.

A world in which a man could come upon such a hunt, himself! What kind of a man?

Rosalind rested her hand on my arm. Sophie looked up. When she saw my face her expression changed.

"What is it?" she asked.

Rosalind told her. Her eyes widened with horror. She looked from me to Petra, then slowly, bemusedly back to me again. She opened her mouth to speak, but lowered her eyes, leaving the thought unsaid. I looked at Petra, too, then at Sophie, at the rags she wore, and the cave we were in.

"Purity," I said. "The will of the Lord. Honor thy father. . . . Am I supposed to forgive him? Or to try to kill him?"

The answer startled me. I was not aware that I had sent out the thought at large.

"Let him be," came the severe, clear pattern from the Zealand woman. "Your work is to survive. Neither his kind, nor his kind of thinking will survive long. They are the crown of creation, they are ambition fulfilled, they have nowhere more to go. But life is change, that is how it differs from the rocks, change is its very nature.

"The living form defies evolution at its peril, if it does not adapt, it will be broken. The Old People brought down Tribulation, and were broken into fragments by it. Your father and his kind are a part of those fragments. They are determined still that there is a final form to defend. Soon they will attain the stability they strive for, in the only form it is granted—a place among the fossils.

"Whether harsh intolerance and bitter rectitude are the armor worn over fear and disappointment, or whether they are the festival-dress of the sadist, they cover an enemy of the life-force. The difference in kind can be bridged only by self-sacrifice—*his* self-sacrifice, for yours would bridge nothing. So, there is the severance. We have a new world to conquer, they have only a lost cause to lose."

She ceased, leaving me somewhat bemused. Rosalind, too, looked as if she were still catching up on it. Petra seemed bored.

Sophie regarded us curiously. She said, "You give an outsider an uncomfortable feeling. Is it something I could know?"

"Well——" I began, and paused, wondering how to put it.

"She said we're not to bother about my father because he doesn't understand, I think," observed Petra. It seemed a pretty fair summary.

"She . . . ?" Sophie inquired.

I remembered that she knew nothing of the Zealand people.

"Oh, a friend of Petra's," I told her, vaguely.

Sophie was sitting close to the entrance, the rest of us

farther back, out of sight from the ground. Presently she looked out and down.

"There are quite a lot of the men back now—most of them, I should think. Some of them are collected around Gordon's tent, most of the others are drifting that way. He must be back, too."

She went on regarding the scene while she finished the contents of her bowl. Then she put it down beside her. "I'll see what I can find out," she said, and disappeared down the ladder.

She was gone fully an hour. I risked a quick look out once or twice, and could see the spider-man in front of his tent. He seemed to be dividing his men up into parties and instructing them by drawing diagrams in the bare earth.

"What's happening?" I asked Sophie, as she returned. "What's the plan?"

She hesitated, looking doubtful.

"For goodness' sake," I told her, "we *want* your people to win, don't we? But we don't want Michael to get hurt, if it can be helped."

"We're going to ambush them this side of the river," she said.

"Let them get across?"

"There's nowhere to make a stand on the other side," she explained.

I suggested to Michael that he should hang back at the riverside, or, if he could not do that, he might fall off during the crossing and get carried away downstream. He said he'd bear the proposal in mind, but try to think of a less uncomfortable means of delay.

A few minutes later a voice called Sophie's name from below. She whispered:

"Keep back. It's him," and sped across and down the ladder.

After that nothing happened for more than a hour, when the Zealand woman came through again:

"Reply to me, please. We need a sharper reading on you now. Just keep on sending numbers."

Petra responded energetically, as if she had been feeling left out of things lately.

"Enough," the Zealand woman told her. "Wait a moment."

Presently she added: "Better than we hoped. We can cut that estimate by an hour."

Another half-hour went by. I sneaked a few quick glimpses outside. The encampment looked all but deserted now. There was no one to be seen among the shacks but a few older women.

"In sight of the river," Michael reported.

Fifteen or twenty minutes passed. Then Michael again:

"They've muffed it, the fools. We've spotted a couple of them moving on the top of the cliffs. Not that it makes a lot of difference, anyway—that cleft's much too obvious a trap. Council of war now."

The council was evidently brief. In less than ten minutes he was through again:

"Plan. We retreat to cover immediately opposite the cleft. There, at a gap in the cover, we leave half a dozen men occasionally passing and repassing in view to give the impression of more, and light fires to suggest that we are held up. Rest of the force is splitting to make detours and two crossings, one upstream, and one down. We then pincer-in behind the cleft. Better inform, if you can."

The encampment was no great distance behind the river cliffs. It looked likely that we might be caught within the pincers. I very much wished Sophie would return. An hour passed, then: "We're across the river downstream from you. No opposition," Michael told us.

We went on waiting.

Suddenly a gun went off somewhere in the woods, on the left. Three or four more shots followed, then silence, then another two.

A few minutes later a crowd of ragged men with quite a number of women among them came pouring out of the woods, leaving the scene of their intended ambush and making toward the firing. They were a woebegone, miserable lot, a few of them visibly deviants, but most of them looking simply the wrecks of normal human beings. I could not see more than three or four guns in all. The rest had bows, and a number had short spears scabbarded at their backs, as well. The spiderman stood out among them, taller than the rest, and close beside him I could see Sophie, with a bow in her hand. Whatever degree of organization there may have been had clearly disintegrated.

"What's happening?" I asked Michael. "Was that your lot shooting?"

"No. That was the other party. They're trying to draw the Fringes men across their way so that we can come in from the opposite side and take them in the rear."

"They're succeeding," I told him.

The sound of more firing came from the same direction as before. A clamor and shouting broke out. A few spent arrows dropped into the left-hand end of the clearing. Some men came running back out of the trees.

Suddenly there was a strong, clear question:

"You're still safe?"

We were all three lying on the floor in the front part of the cave now. We had a view of what was going on, and there was little enough chance of anyone noticing our heads, or bothering about us if he did. The way things were going was plain even to Petra. She loosed an urgent, excited flash.

"Steady, child, steady! We're coming," admonished the Zealand woman.

More arrows fell into the left-hand end of the clearing, and more ragged figures appeared in rapid retreat. They ran back, dodging as they came, and took cover among the tents and hovels. Still more followed, with arrows spitting out of the woods after them. The Fringes men crouched behind their bits of cover, bobbing up now and then to take quick shots at figures scarcely visible between the trees.

Unexpectedly a shower of arrows flew in from the other end of the clearing. The tattered men and women discovered themselves to be between two fires, and started to panic. Most of them jumped to their feet and ran for the shelter of the caves. I got ready to push the ladder away if any of them should try to climb into ours.

Half a dozen horsemen appeared, riding out of the trees on the right. I noticed the spider-man. He was standing by his tent, bow in hand, watching the riders. Sophie, beside him, was tugging at his ragged jacket, urging him to run toward the caves. He brushed her back with his long right arm, never taking his eyes from the emerging horsemen. His right hand went back to the string, and held the bow half-drawn. His eyes kept on searching among the horsemen.

Suddenly he stiffened. His bow came up like a flash, bent to its full. He loosed. The shaft took my father in the left of his chest. He jerked, and fell back on Sheba's hindquarters. Then he slithered off sideways and dropped to the ground, his right foot still caught in the stirrup.

The spider-man threw down his bow, and turned. With a scoop of his long arms he snatched up Sophie, and began to run. His spindly legs had not made more than three prodigious strides when a couple of arrows took him simultaneously in the back and side, and he fell.

Sophie struggled to her feet and began to run on by herself. An arrow pierced right through her upper arm, but she held on, with it lodged there. Then another took her in the back of the neck. She dropped in mid-stride, and her body slid along in the dust.

Petra had not seen it happen. She was looking all around, with a bewildered expression.

"What's that?" she asked. "What's that queer noise?"

The Zealand woman came in, calm, confidence-inspiring.

"Don't be frightened. We're coming. It's all right. Stay just where you are."

I could hear the noise now. A strange drumming sound, gradually swelling. One could not place it; it seemed to be filling everywhere, emanating from nowhere.

More men were coming out of the woods into the clearing, most of them on horseback. Many of them I recognized, men I had known all my life, all joined together now to hunt us down.

Suddenly one of the horsemen shouted and pointed upward.

I looked up, too. The sky was no longer clear. Something like a bank of mist, but shot with quick iridescent flashes, hung over us. Above it, as if through a veil, I could make out one of the strange, fish-shaped craft that I had dreamt of in my childhood, hanging in the sky. The mist made it indistinct in detail, but what I could see of it was just as I remembered: a white, glistening body with something half-invisible whizzing around above it. It was growing bigger and louder as it dropped toward us.

As I looked down again I saw a few glistening threads, like cobwebs, drifting past the mouth of the cave. Then more and more of them, giving sudden gleams as they twisted in the air and caught the light.

The shooting fell off. All over the clearing the invaders lowered their bows and guns and stared upward. They goggled incredulously, then those on the left jumped to their feet with shouts of alarm, and turned to run. Over on the right the horses pranced with fright, whinnied, and began to bolt in all directions. In a few seconds the whole place was in chaos. Fleeing men caromed into one another, panic-stricken horses trampled through the flimsy shacks, and tripped on the guy-ropes of tents flinging their riders headlong.

I sought for Michael.

"Here!" I told him. "This way. Come along over here."

"Coming," he told me.

I spotted him then, just getting to his feet beside a fallen horse that was kicking out violently. He looked up toward our cave, found us, and waved a hand. He turned to glance up at the machine in the sky. It was still sinking gently down, perhaps a couple of hundred feet above us now. Underneath it the queer mist eddied in a great swirl.

"Coming," repeated Michael.

He turned toward us and started. Then he paused and picked at something on his arm. His hand stayed there.

"Queer," he told us. "Like a cobweb, but sticky. I can't get my hand——" His thought suddenly became panicky. "It's stuck. I can't move it!"

The Zealand woman came in, coolly advising:

"Don't struggle. You'll exhaust yourself. Lie down if you can. Keep calm. Don't move. Just wait. Keep your back on the ground so that it can't get *around* you."

I saw Michael obey the instruction, though his thoughts were by no means confident. Suddenly, I realized that all over the clearing men were clawing at themselves, trying to get the stuff off, but where their hands touched it they stuck. They were struggling with it like flies in treacle, and all the time more strands were floating down on them. Most of them fought with it for a few seconds and then tried to run for shelter of the trees. They'd take about three steps before their feet stuck together, and they pitched on to the ground. The threads already lying there trapped them further. More threads fell lightly down on them as they struggled and thrashed about until presently they could struggle no more. The horses were no better off. I saw one back into a small bush. When it moved forward it tore the bush out by the roots. The bush swung round and touched the other hind leg. The legs became inseparable. The horse fell over and lay kicking—for a while.

A descending strand wafted across the back of my own hand. I told Rosalind and Petra to get back into the cave. I looked at the strand, not daring to touch it with my other hand. I turned the hand over slowly and carefully and tried to scrape the stuff off on the rock. I was not careful enough. The movement brought the strand, and other strands, looping slowly toward me, and my hand was glued to the rock.

"Here they are," Petra cried, in words and thoughts together.

I looked up to see the gleaming white fish-shape settling into the middle of the clearing. Its descent swirled the floating filaments in a cloud about it and thrust a waft of air outward. I saw some of the strands in front of the cave-mouth hesitate, undulate and then come drifting inward. Involuntarily I closed my eyes. There was a light gossamer touch on my face. When I tried to open my eyes again I found I could not.

Chapter Seventeen

IT NEEDS a lot of resolution to lie perfectly still while you feel more and more sticky strands falling with a feathery, tickling touch across your face and hands; and still more when you begin to feel those which landed first press on your skin like fine cords and tug gently at it.

I caught Michael wondering with some alarm if this was not a trick, and whether he might not have been better off if he had tried to run. Before I could reply the Zealand woman came in reassuring us again, telling us to keep calm and have patience. Rosalind emphasized that to Petra.

"Has it got you, too?" I asked her.

"Yes," she said. "The wind from the machine blew it right into the cave—Petra, darling, you heard what she said. You must try to keep still."

The throbbing and the whirring that had dominated everything grew less as the machine slowed down. Presently it stopped. The succeeding silence was shocking. There were a few half-muffled calls and smothered sounds, but little more. I understood the reasons for that. Strands had fallen across my own mouth. I could not have opened it to call out if I wanted to.

The waiting seemed interminable. My skin crawled under the touch of the stuff, and the pull of it was becoming painful.

The Zealand woman inquired: "Michael? Keep counting to guide me to you."

Michael started counting, in figure-shapes. They were steady until the one and the two of his twelve wavered and dissolved into a pattern of relief and thankfulness. In the silence that had now fallen I could hear him say in words, "They're in that cave there, that one."

There was a creak from the ladder, a gritting of its poles

against the ledge, and presently a slight hissing noise. A dampness fell on my face and hands, and the skin began to lose its puckered feeling. I tried to open my eyes again; they resisted, but gave slowly. There was a sticky feeling about the lids as I raised them.

Close in front of me, standing on the upper rungs of the ladder and leaning inward, was a figure entirely hidden in a shiny white suit. There were still filaments leisurely adrift in the air, but when they fell on the headpiece or shoulders of the white suit they did not stick. They slithered off and wafted gently on their downward way. I could see nothing of the suit's wearer but a pair of eyes looking at me through small, transparent windows. In a white gloved hand was a metal bottle, with a fine spray hissing from it.

"Turn over," came the woman's thought.

I turned, and she played the spray up and down the front of my clothes. Then she climbed the last two or three rungs, stepped over me where I lay, and made her way toward Rosalind and Petra at the back of the cave, spraying as she went.

Michael's head and shoulders appeared above the sill. He, too, was bedewed with spray, and the few vagrant strands that settled on him lay glistening for a moment before they dissolved. I sat up and looked past him.

The white machine rested in the middle of the clearing. The device on top of it had ceased to revolve, and now that it was observable, seemed to be a sort of conical spiral, built up in a number of spaced sections from some almost transparent material. There were glazed windows in the side of the fish-shaped body, and a door stood open.

The clearing itself looked as if a fantastic number of spiders had spun there with all their might and main. The place was festooned with threads, appearing more white than glossy now; it took a moment or two of feeling something was wrong with them before one perceived that they failed to move in the breeze as webs would. And not only they, but everything, was motionless, petrified.

The forms of a number of men, and horses, too, were scattered among the shacks. They were as unmoving as the rest.

A sudden sharp cracking came from the right. I looked

over there, just in time to see a young tree break off a foot from the ground, and fall. Then another movement caught the corner of my eye—a bush slowly leaning over. Its roots came out of the ground as I watched. Another bush moved. A shack crumpled in on itself and collapsed, and another. It was uncanny and alarming.

Back in the cave there was a sigh of relief from Rosalind. I got up and went to her, with Michael following. Petra announced in a subdued, somewhat expostulatory tone, "That was *very* horrid."

Her eyes dwelt reprovingly and curiously on the white-suited figure. The woman made a few final, all-encompassing passes with her spray, then pulled off her gloves and lifted back her hood. She regarded us. We frankly stared at her.

Her eyes were large, with irises more brown than green, and fringed with long, deep-gold lashes. Her nose was straight, but her nostrils curved with the perfection of a sculpture. Her mouth was perhaps a little wide; the chin beneath it was rounded, but not soft. Her hair was just a little darker than Rosalind's, and, astonishingly in a woman, it was short. Cut off nearly level with her jaw.

But more than anything it was the lightness of her face that made us stare. It was not pallor, it was simply fairness, like new cream, and with cheeks that might have been dusted with pink petals. There was scarcely a line in its smoothness, it seemed all new and perfect, as if neither wind nor rain had ever touched her. It was hard to believe that any real, living person could look like that, so untouched, so unflawed.

For she was no girl in a first tender blossoming, unmistakably she was a woman—thirty, perhaps; one could not tell. She was sure of herself, with a serenity of confidence which made Rosalind's self-reliance seem almost bravado.

She took us in and then fixed her attention upon Petra. She smiled at her, with just a glimpse of perfect, white teeth.

There was an immensely complex pattern which compounded pleasure, satisfaction, achievement, relief, approval, and most surprisingly to me a touch of something very like awe. The intermixture was subtle far beyond Petra's grasp, but enough of it reached her to give her an unwonted, wide-eyed seriousness for some seconds as she looked up into the woman's eyes, as if she knew in some way, without understanding how or why, that this was one of the cardinal moments in her life.

Then, after a few moments, her expression relaxed. She smiled and chuckled. Evidently something was passing between them, but it was of a quality, or on a level, that did not reach me at all. I caught Rosalind's eye, but she simply shook her head, and watched.

The Zealand woman bent down and picked Petra up. They looked closely into one another's faces. Petra raised her hand and tentatively touched the woman's face, as if to assure herself that it was real. The Zealand woman laughed, kissed her, and put her down again. She shook her head slowly, as if she were not quite believing.

"It was worthwhile," she said, in words, but words so curiously pronounced that I scarcely understood them at first. "Yes. Certainly, it was worthwhile!"

She slipped into thought-forms, much easier to follow than her words.

"It was not simple to get permission to come. Such an immense distance, more than twice as far as any of us has been before. So costly to send the ship. They could scarcely believe it would be worth it. But it will be. . . ." She looked at Petra again, wonderingly. "At her age, and untrained—yet she can throw a thought halfway round the world!" She shook her head once more, as if still unable to believe it entirely. Then she turned to me.

"She has still a great deal to learn, but we will give her the best teachers, and then, one day, she will be teaching them."

She sat down on Sophie's bed of twigs and skins. Against the thrown-back white hood, her beautiful head looked as though it were framed by a halo. She studied each of us thoughtfully in turn, and seemed satisfied. She nodded.

"With one another's help, you have managed to get quite a long way, too; but you'll find that there is a lot more we can teach you." She took hold of Petra's hand. "Well, as you've no possessions to collect, and there's nothing to delay us, we might as well start now."

"For Waknuk?" Michael asked.

It was as much a statement as a question, and she checked herself in the act of rising, to look at him inquiringly.

"There is still Deborah," he explained.

The Zealand woman considered.

"I'm not sure—— Wait a minute," she told him.

She was suddenly in communication with someone on board the machine outside, at a speed and on a level where I could make almost nothing of it. Presently she shook her head, regretfully.

"I was afraid of that," she said. "I am sorry, but we cannot include her."

"It wouldn't take long. It isn't far, not for your flying-machine," Michael insisted.

Again she shook her head.

"I am sorry," she said again. "Of course we would if we could, but it is a technical matter. You see, the journey was longer than we expected. There were some dreadful parts that we dare not cross, even at great height: we had to go far around them. Also, because of what was happening here, we had to come faster than we had intended." She paused, seeming to wonder whether she was attempting an explanation beyond the understanding of such primitives as we. "The machine," she told us, "uses fuel. The more weight it has to carry, and the faster it travels, the more of this fuel it uses, and now we have only just enough of it left to get us back, if we go carefully. If we were to go to Waknuk and make another landing and take-off there, *and* try to carry four of you, as well as Petra, we should use up all our fuel before we could reach home. That would mean that we should fall into the sea, and drown. Three of you from here we can just manage with safety; four and the extra landing, we can't."

There was a pause while we appreciated the situation. She had made it clear enough, and she sat back, a motionless figure in her gleaming white suit, her knees drawn up and her hands clasped around them, waiting sympathetically and patiently for us to accept the facts.

In the pause one became aware of the uncanniness of the silence all about us. There was not a sound to be heard now. Not a movement. Even the leaves on the trees were unable to rustle. A sudden shock of realization brought a question from Rosalind:

"They're not—they're not all—dead? I didn't understand. I thought——"

"Yes," the Zealand woman told her, simply. "They're all dead. The plastic threads contract as they dry. A man who struggles and entangles himself soon becomes unconscious. It is more merciful than your arrows and spears."

Rosalind shivered. Perhaps I did, too. There was an unnerving quality about it—something quite different from the fatal issue of a man-to-man fight, or from the casualty roll of an ordinary battle. We were puzzled, too, by the Zealand woman, for there was no callousness in her mind, nor any great concern, either—just a slight distaste, as if for an unavoidable, but unexceptional, necessity. She perceived our confusion, and shook her head reprovingly.

"It is not pleasant to kill any creature," she agreed, "but to pretend that one can live without doing so is self-deception. There has to be meat in the dish, there have to be vegetables forbidden to flower, seeds forbidden to germinate; even the cycles of microbes must be sacrificed for us to continue our cycles. It is neither shameful nor shocking that it should be so. It is simply a part of the great revolving wheel of natural economy. And just as we have to keep ourselves alive in these ways, so, too, we have to preserve our species against others that wish to destroy it, or else fail in our trust.

"The unhappy Fringes people were condemned through no act of their own to a life of squalor and misery—there could be no future for them. As for those who condemned them—well, that, too, is the way of it. There have been lords of life before, you know. Did you ever hear of the great lizards? When the time came for them to be superseded they had to pass away.

"Sometime there will come a day when we ourselves shall have to give place to a new thing. Very certainly we shall struggle against the inevitable just as these remnants of the Old People do. We shall try with all our strength to grind it back into the earth from which it is emerging, for treachery to one's own species must always seem a crime. We shall force it to prove itself, and when it does, we shall go; as, by the same process, these are going.

"In loyalty to their kind they cannot tolerate our rise; in loyalty to our kind, we cannot tolerate their obstruction.

"If the process shocks you, it is because you have not been able to stand off and, knowing what you are, see what a difference in *kind* must mean. Your minds are confused by your ties and your upbringing, you are still half-thinking of them as the same kind as yourselves. That is why you are shocked. And that is why they have you at a disadvantage, for *they* are not confused. They are alert, corporately aware of danger to their species. They can see quite well that if it is to survive they have not only to preserve it from deterioration, but they must protect it from the even more serious threat of the superior variant.

"For ours *is* a superior variant, and we are only just beginning. We are able to think-together and understand one another as they never could; we are beginning to understand how to assemble and apply the composite team-mind to a problem, and where may that not take us one day? We are not shut away into individual cages from which we can reach out only with inadequate words. Understanding one another, we do not need laws which treat living forms as though they were as indistinguishable as bricks; we could never commit the enormity of imagining that we could mint ourselves into equality and identity, like stamped coins; we do not mechanistically attempt to hammer ourselves into geometrical patterns of society, or policy; we are not dogmatists teaching God how he should have ordered the world.

"The essential quality of life is living; the essential quality of living is change; change is evolution; and we are part of it.

"The static, the enemy of change, is the enemy of life, and therefore our implacable enemy. If you still feel shocked, or doubtful, just consider some of the things that these people who have taught you to think of them as your fellows, have done. I know little about your lives, but the pattern scarcely varies wherever a pocket of the older species is trying to preserve itself. And consider, too, what they intended to do to you, and why."

I found her rhetorical style somewhat overwhelming, but,

in general, I was able to follow her line of thought. I did not have the power of detachment that could allow me to think of myself as another species, nor am I sure that I have it yet. In my thinking we were still no more than unhappy minor variants; but I could look back and consider why we had been forced to flee.

I glanced at Petra. She was sitting pretty much bored with all this apologia, watching the Zealand woman's beautiful face with a kind of wistful wonder. A series of memories cut off what my eyes were seeing—my Aunt Harriet's face in the water, her hair gently waving in the current; poor Anne, a limp figure hanging from a beam; Sally, wringing her hands in anguish for Katherine, and in terror for herself; Sophie, degraded to a savage, dying with an arrow in her neck. . . .

Any of those might have been a picture of Petra's future.

I shifted over beside her, and put an arm around her.

During all the Zealand woman's disquisition Michael had been gazing out of the entrance, running his eyes almost covetously over the machine that waited in the clearing. He went on studying it for a minute or two after she had stopped, then he sighed, and turned away. For a few moments he contemplated the rock floor between his feet. Presently he looked up.

"Petra," he asked, "do you think you could reach Deborah for me?"

Petra put out the inquiry, in her forceful way.

"Yes. She's there. She wants to know what's happening," she told him.

"Say first that whatever she may hear, we're all alive and quite all right."

"Yes," said Petra presently. "She understands that."

"Now I want you tell her this," Michael went on, carefully. "She is to go on being brave—and very careful—and in a little time, three or four days, perhaps, I shall come and fetch her away. Will you tell her that?"

All of us looked at Michael, without open comment.

"Well," he said, defensively, "you two are proscribed as outlaws, so neither of you can go."

"But, Michael——" Rosalind began.

"She's quite *alone,*" said Michael. "Would you leave David alone there, or would David leave you?"

There was no answer to that.

"You said 'fetch her away,' " observed Rosalind.

"That's what I meant. We *could* stay in Waknuk for a while, waiting for the day when we, or perhaps our children, would be found out. . . . That's not good enough. Or we could come to the Fringes." He looked around the cave and out across the clearing, with distaste. "That's not good enough, either. Deborah deserves just as well as any of the rest of us. All right, then; since the machine can't take her, someone's got to bring her."

The Zealand woman was leaning forward, watching him. There was sympathy and admiration in her eyes, but she shook her head gently.

"It is a very long way—and there's that awful, impassable country in between," she reminded him.

"I know that," he acknowledged. "But the world is round. so there must be another way to get there."

"It would be hard, and certainly dangerous," she warned.

"No more dangerous than to stay in Waknuk. Besides, how could we stay now, knowing that there is a place for people like us, that there *is* somewhere to go?

"*Knowing* makes all the difference. Knowing that we're not just pointless freaks—a few bewildered Deviations hoping to save their own skins. It's the difference between just trying to keep alive, and having something to live for."

The Zealand woman thought for a moment or two, then she raised her eyes to meet his again.

"When you do reach us, Michael," she told him. "You can be very sure of your place with us."

The door shut with a thud. The machine started to vibrate and blow a great dusty wind across the clearing. Through the windows we could see Michael bracing himself against it, his clothes flapping. Even the deviational trees about the clearing were stirring in their webby shrouds.

The floor tilted beneath us. There was a slight lurch, then the ground began to drop away as we climbed faster and faster into the evening sky. Soon we steadied, pointed toward the southwest.

Petra was excited, and a bit over strength.

"It's awfully wonderful," she announced. "I can see for simply miles and miles and miles. Oh, Michael, you do look funny and tiny down there!"

The lone, miniature figure in the clearing waved its arm.

"Just at present," Michael's thought came up to us, "I seem to be feeling a bit funny and tiny down here, Petra, dear. But it'll pass. We'll be coming after you."

It was just as I had seen it in my dreams. A brighter sun than Waknuk ever knew poured down upon the wide blue bay where the lines of white-topped breakers crawled slowly to the beach. Small boats, some with colored sails, and some with none, were making for a harbor already dotted with craft. Clustered along the shore, and thinning as it stretched back toward the hills, lay the city with its white houses embedded among green parks and gardens. I could even make out the tiny vehicles sliding along the wide, tree-bordered avenues. A little inland, beside a square of green, a bright light was blinking from a tower and a fish-shaped machine was floating to the ground.

It was so familiar that for a swift moment I imagined I should wake to find myself back in my bed in Waknuk. I took hold of Rosalind's hand to reassure myself.

"It *is* real, isn't it? You can see it, too?" I asked her.

"It's beautiful, David. I never thought there could be anything so lovely. . . . And there's something else, too, that you never told me about."

"What?" I asked.

"Listen! Can't you feel it? Open your mind more.—Petra, darling, if you *could* stop bubbling over for a few minutes. . . ."

I did as she told me. I was aware of the engineer in our machine communicating with someone below, but behind that, as a background to it, there was something new and unknown to me. In terms of sound it could be not unlike the buzzing of a hive of bees; in terms of light, a suffused glow.

"What is it?" I said, puzzled.

"Can't you guess, David? It's people. Lots and lots of our kind of people."

I realized she must be right, and I listened to it for a bit, until Petra's excitement got the better of her, and I had to protect myself.

We were over the land now, and looked down at the city coming up to meet us.

"I'm beginning to believe it's real and true at last," I told Rosalind. "You were never with me those other times."

She turned her head. The under-Rosalind was in her face, smiling, shiny-eyed. The armor was gone. She let me look beneath. It was like a flower opening. . . .

"This time, David——" she began.

Then she was blotted out. We staggered, and put our hands to our heads. Even the floor under our feet jerked a little.

Anguished protests came from all directions.

"Oh, sorry," Petra apologized to the ship's crew, and to the city in general, "but it *is* awfully exciting."

"This time, darling, we'll forgive you," Rosalind told her. "It *is*."